SUICIDE

BY RUSTY HODGDON

OTHER NOVELS BY RUSTY HODGDON

~ THE SUBWAY KILLER

Anthony Johnson is a handsome, charismatic pimp who is suspected of murdering several college co-eds. When Mark Bowden, a young, impressionable Public Defender is assigned to represent him, he quickly finds himself cajoled by the beautiful women of Johnson's stable into going far beyond the bounds of ethical legal conduct.

~ INSANITY

The denizens of a small town in California start engaging in strange, aberrant behavior. When a young health inspector begins to suspect the cause could be attributed to the spillage of an hallucinogetic chemical into the town's water supply, his efforts to disclose that fact expose him to possible fatal retribution.

~THE EYE

A monstrous hurricane forms in Africa, ravages the Cape Verdes, and strikes Bermuda and the Florida coast. Some of the characters believe it is following them in retribution for past sins. Of course, it isn't . . . or is it? This psychological thriller will keep you riveted . . . and squirming.

~THE PHANTOM WRITER

Ian Anderson is past his prime as a mystery writer. His publisher delivers an ultimatum—take on a ghost writer or we'll drop you. A beautiful, young woman is hired and submits a superlative manuscript. Ian secretly adopts it as his own and finds out the plot describes a real-life crime—with details only the perpetrator would know. How does he explain that?

~SELFIE

A young girl is found raped and murdered near the Salt Ponds in Key West. A young attorney is appointed to represent the accused. The evidence stacks up against his client, until he discovers a selfie photograph the defendant took near the scene that seems to show two others disposing of the body. What follows next is a twisted, demented tale of police corruption and cover-up.

This book is a work of fiction. Names, characters, places and incidents are products of the author's over-active imagination or are used fictitiously. Any resemblance to actual events or locales or persons, living or dead, is entirely coincidental.

All rights reserved, including the right to reproduce this book or portions thereof in any form whatsoever.

Published by Rusty Hodgdon

2012

There is but one truly philosophical problem, and that is suicide.
<u>Albert Camus</u> (1913-1960). *The Myth of Sisyphus*

* * * * *

I wild my breast and sore my pride,
I bask in dreams of suicide,
If cool my heart and high my head
I think "How lucky are the dead."
<u>Dorothy Parker</u> (1893-1967)

[ONE]

At first blush, you might say the whole sordid mess began in the early morning hours of a hot, muggy Saturday in August. That's when I was taking my morning jog along South Roosevelt and Smathers Beach. But as I learned later, it actually started two nights before, at Jack's Sports Bar on Duval. I'd gone there almost every night since I arrived in Key West just over a month before. Greatest sports bar in the universe, if you ask me. But I guess no one's asking.

Not only do they have the usual mix of large projection and small flat screens, but they also provide those neat little audio boxes that you can set in front of you and tune in the sound for the screen you're watching. When you've recently left your career of twenty-five years, and a marriage of slightly more, sports, not to mention the Keys, are a great way to get away from it.

In any event, I was just sitting there that night, minding my own goddamn business, when this guy plops down next to me at the bar. I wouldn't have noticed anything if there hadn't been three free stools right next to him. Maybe you're like me, but I have this spatial sixth sense. I know when someone has unnecessarily invaded my personal geography. It's that slight, uneasy feeling you get in your gut. Danger close by.

Suicide

He also started up a conversation a little too quickly. Definitely got my gay-dar flashing. Need to be careful of that in the Conch Republic. An intelligent guy. Knew his baseball. The races were heating up in late summer. I was a Cubs fan all the way. That's a team that can get the juices going both ways—love and hate. Key West doesn't have any pro baseball teams, unless you count the Rays or the Marlins, which nobody does. This is a town of outsiders.

It was when his hand lingered a little too long on my shoulder that I had to say something. Something easy-going, like, "Get your fucking hands off me, asshole," combined with a turn and a shrug that forced the hand off. Needless to say, I'd had a little too much to drink. That cheap Yuengling will get you every time.

"Hey, what's the matter with you, man?" he said.

"I just don't like people touchin' me, that's all."

"It was just a friendly gesture, for God's sake. Get over it."

"I'll get over whatever I goddamn well feel like gettin' over." I was slurring my words a little now. I got up and left, carefully sliding off the opposite end of the stool so as not to brush by him.

"Catch ya later, chief," I said with a bit of disdain in my voice As I got to the door, I was vaguely aware that someone was following me out. I caught the reflection of my new "friend" in the glass door panel. Deciding to have the confrontation outside, rather than in—and I was sure there was going to be one—I pushed through and didn't turn around until I was on the sidewalk. It was early evening, and still very hot, so only a few pedestrians populated the streets. Sure enough, as I turned, he was right there, in my face.

"Look, asshole." It was him speaking. Guess I was the asshole now.

"I don't like your attitude one bit. You should be a little friendlier. This is a laid-back place."

I don't know what possessed me. I really don't. Maybe I just wasn't that laid back yet. I punched him smack in the face. He was quick enough to dodge the brunt of it, but I had opened a gash above his left eye. Must've been my college ring. I had only recently gotten into the habit of wearing it again. He swung back, but I was ready, and easily blocked it with my forearm. At that instant, two burly guys came busting through the doors—I later learned they were bouncing for the bar—and pushed us apart.

The typical posturing between us started, each of us obviously knowing—and honestly, relieved—that the fight was over.

Him: "I'll take care of you later on."

Suicide

Me: "Yeah, right, ya faggot." And so on. I took off north toward the Lazy Lizard, another of my now favorite watering holes. Doing a mental post mortem of the entire affair, I concluded I had been intentionally provoked. The guy was clearly trying to get a rise out of me. And I took the bait.

What was the matter with me? Here in my late fifties, and getting into bar fights? That hadn't happened to me since college, many moons ago. Why was this anger, this impatience rising poisonously to the surface now? I really didn't like the person I had become.

My self-analysis lasted to the doors of the Lizard. I spent the rest of the night squelching any further introspection.

[TWO]

The next morning the reality of my predicament came rushing in—as did the waves of nausea. I had to admit, hangovers at fifty-eight are as bad as bar fights.

I had left the marriage because I was getting bored. Plain and simple. My ex was not a bad woman. She had just gotten old beyond her years and conservative as the years went by. I'm not proud of it.

I had been in real estate for a quarter of a century. Was pretty good at it. Mostly residential, but some commercial, some new developments. I had seen a lot of booms and busts. Had weathered them all until this last one. This was the worst by far. When I gave up the farm in the divorce: the house, the time share, most of the retirement—what little was left after the collapse—I decided to give up the business, and move as far away as possible. Coming from Wisconsin, the Florida Keys made a good candidate.

I had always loved writing. Was an English major in college, took a lot of creative writing courses. One professor lauded a short story I had written, even read it to the class. Took a whole period. But somehow the weight of life—marriage, job, three kids—sublimated the artistic juices. I would sit down

Suicide

on occasion to start something—an idea for a story already stewing—and nothing would come out. I'd heard of writer's cramp—this was more like rigor mortis.

So after abandoning a marriage, then a career, I decided to give it one more try. I did an initial reconnoiter. Key West seemed the ideal place to start. The town oozed creativity. I took a tour of the Ernest Hemingway house, and was deeply moved. The beauty of the surroundings, of his writing loft, inspired me. I read almost all of his works over the ensuing months after that first trip. I knew I had to go back.

So here I was, still staring at the blank page on my laptop screen. Yeah, I had the title page. And the next page that started with "Chapter One." Oh, and I had a great story to write. I had read about this town in California where, inexplicably, all kinds of horrible, strange things were going on. A young Sunday school teacher raped and murdered a friend's minor daughter. A doctor was convicted of numerous sexual assaults on his patients. A teenage boy was held captive by some relatives and, after escaping, showed up at a school gym, filthy, emaciated, and in chains. I was going to cast the reality of the events into a fictional narrative with an imagined explanation for the carnage—the escape of a potent, hallucinogenic drug into the water system.

<u>Rusty Hodgdon</u>

But I couldn't get out a single sentence. I tried typing a word on the screen—any word—to see if that would prompt me to create a story around it. Didn't work. My frustration level was mounting daily, hourly, by the minute. I was getting nasty. When my children called me, I barked at them over small things. Their calls became less frequent. My drinking was getting out of hand. My impatience showed too easily in last night's encounter. I had to turn things around.

Of course, Hemingway's suicide at age sixty-one—heck, I was only a few years away from that myself—began to weigh heavily on me. He blew his head off with a shotgun after receiving electroshock treatments at the Mayo Clinic. No one knew back then what horrors that procedure could wreak. Found he couldn't write. Not a single word. Death was a better alternative that creative muteness.

I knew how he must have felt.

THREE

That's why I decided to take up jogging. Never really done it seriously before. Before coming down to the Keys, I had joined a gym for a couple of months and used the treadmill. That's about it.

I knew I had to have something to get me up and going in the morning. It was impossible to run after nine am in August in the Key West. The sun was just too intense. So I rousted myself up and out of bed at seven—despite anything that had happened the night before—pulled on my shorts, T-shirt and shoes and ventured out. After a week, I found it was beginning to clear my head, the poison being sweat out and released from my body. I was staying at a small bungalow apartment on Atlantic Boulevard near Bertha. It was a short distance to South Roosevelt and the beach. My distance increased almost daily. First to the Fort East Martello Museum and back, a distance of about two miles. Then past the airport; next onto Flagler; and on the return, past my place to Higgs Beach, and finally, Southernmost Point.

It worked up to a point. I was feeling better. But the booze and the increasing depression were a powerful counterpoint, and I vacillated between states of mild contentment and

Rusty Hodgdon

deep despair. Little did I know that the events of that Saturday would take me to new, and more extreme, levels of the two.

FOUR

I had arisen particularly early that morning committed to taking a jog. Avoiding the sauce the night before made that easier. After the confrontation of two nights before I had decided it was time to cool the jets.

The sun had yet to expose itself over Stock Island when I started out. The temperature was just right—low eighties, with a slight decrease in humidity. Soon after I turned the corner onto Roosevelt and hit the ocean, a light breeze quickly dried the sheen of sweat that had developed as soon as I had walked out the door. I remember being in very good spirits. This may have been the turning point I was looking for.

I ran smoothly and easily along the beach, admiring, as always, the slight rustling of the palms that grew down toward the sea. I had not yet hit the stench of the seaweed that was omnipresent further east at this time of year.

I passed none of the usual straggling joggers and bicyclists this early. I had the world to myself. There were rarely any cars parked along South Roosevelt at any time in the morning, so I was a bit surprised to see a SUV, a Jeep, parked alongside the road with its engine running. The windows were darkly tinted in the back and sides, as is common in Florida, so I could not see immediately into the interior. I was surprised enough to take a backward glance through the front windshield, which was more transparent. Although the glass reflected the first rays of light creeping over the horizon, I could still clearly see someone—it appeared to be a man-- in the driver's seat. And in an instant, I saw something else—a metallic object glinted back at me. The person inside was holding the object to the side of his head in such a way that his intent was unmistakable. There is something about the awkwardness of the angle of the arm when someone is putting a gun to his head that immediately broadcasts his purpose.

My first instinct, of course, was to run faster away from the scene, a source of danger, of extreme disturbance. But something in me—maybe a little more reckless disregard for my own safety now that I was divorced and my children grown—caused me to stop. Should I approach the vehicle, or yell at the individual inside, or try to flag down a passing car, of which there were none? My decision-making process was short-lived. The roar of the blast inside the car was at first surprising, what with all the windows closed, but I quickly understood that the sound of the gun shot was combined with the crashing puncture of the driver's window on the other side as the bullet exited the man's head and sprayed shatter proof glass across the roadway.

Again, I don't know what possessed me. I had jumped

involuntarily at the sound of the gunshot. Then my fight or flight instinct took over. But this time I decided to fight—fight past my fear of the danger that so clearly presented itself, the fear of getting involved. I carefully approached the vehicle, keeping my eyes intently on the figure inside. I couldn't see any details, but the person was no longer moving—My primary concern, as there was a gun involved—and appeared to be slumped over toward the driver's door.

Looking around for anyone, a car, a passer-by, to afford me some support, and there was no one, I stepped carefully to the front passenger window and looked in. It indeed was a male, and from all appearances, he was quite dead. I detected no motion, not the slow rise of his chest from what should have been his breathing, not the flutter of an eyelid. Blood, and I guess what you would call gore—a greenish, yellowish ooze—were dripping down what remained of the driver's window.

To this day I don't know why I did what I did. I guess I wanted to see if there was a possibility that the person was alive so I might offer what assistance I could. There was no one else around, and I hadn't brought my cell phone. I opened the passenger door slowly, leaned inside, and felt for a pulse on the man's wrist. There was nothing. In the process, my hand came into contact with a hard, cold object lying on the seat. I grasped it, not realizing it was a gun until I had literally lifted it into my line of vision.

I know now I shouldn't have picked it up. But I did. Once I did, I had no place to put it. I wasn't going to put it back in that crap in the car. Nor was I going to drop it, for fear it would go off. So I held it. In fact, that's where it was—right in my hand—when the first cop car came screaming up to the scene.

I had forgotten it was there, if you can believe it. I don't remember much of those first few minutes. An officer jumped out of his vehicle, gun drawn, and demanded that I drop it immediately. Which I finally did . . . carefully. When he yelled for me to get down on my stomach with my hands behind my head, I was really pissed—I was still standing on a hard, concrete sidewalk, which was getting hotter by the second. I started to complain—that I had just come to the aid of the man who had shot himself—when the cop fired a warning shot in the air. I hit the deck without any thought of what the impact might do to me.

Before I could feel the pain in my body from the fall, two more cruisers did power slides into the area. To my absolute chagrin, and despite my manifold protestations, I was rudely handcuffed and roughly packed in the back of one of the cars.

One of the officers asked me briefly what I was doing there, what had happened. I tried to answer him as honestly as I could, but that questioning ended quickly when the homicide detectives arrived. There were two of them—they introduced

Suicide

themselves as Detective Reilly and Detective Santos, and showed me their badges. Toward Santos—and for the life of me I don't know why I did it—I suddenly blurted out, "You don't need no stinkin' badges." I think the steady diet of alcohol must have gotten to me.

Strangely, they didn't think it was all that funny. They pulled me out of the car, bent me over the hood, and began the interrogation in earnest. I had seen enough TV shows and cop movies to know the good cop-bad cop act when I saw it. I also knew that repetitive inquiries, devoted to catching me in a lie, were the norm. Again, I responded as best I could. I was still shaking from the whole ordeal. And looking back—and yes hindsight is twenty-twenty—I wish I hadn't said I had never seen the man before, because in reality his visage was covered with such a mess that I had no way of knowing one way or the other.

FIVE

Eventually they appeared to be reasonably satisfied with my answers, and removed the cuffs and let me go, but not without an earnest admonition not to leave the city. I walked—not jogged—back to my place. I was exhausted. I lay down in bed and fell asleep for about an hour. When I awoke I was full of a sudden sense of urgency, of unfocused energy. I moved about the apartment doing small chores, picking up dirty clothes, empty bottles of various descriptions, rotting plates of food. Within an hour the place was spotless for the first time since I had arrived.

Looking about for something else to do, I spotted the computer, untouched for weeks. Sitting down and firing it up, I turned to the title page, and began to write. An avalanche of thoughts, ideas, concepts, flooded my mind. My fingers could barely keep up. I sat there all day, only getting up once or twice to stretch my legs and use the bathroom, and pounded out the words. By nine o'clock, every bone in my body aching, I had finished twenty-seven pages and five chapters. I showered, went to bed, and slept like a baby.

That harmonious state was abruptly interrupted by a loud knocking at the front door at six am. I struggled to consciousness, pulled on some shorts and a clean T-shirt, and looked through the small glass pane in the door. It was Reilly and Santos. They looked disheveled, as if they hadn't slept all night, and very impatient. Santos yelled, "Open the fuckin' door, Hunter!"

I was in no mood for this, but knew better than to put them off. The thought of demanding to have an attorney with me briefly crossed my mind, but that would involve a lot of effort, and I wanted to get this over with as soon as possible. I wasn't guilty of anything, except being in the wrong place at the wrong time. That had happened before, and I was still breathing.

I opened the door and let them in. Reilly and I sat down, cater-corner from each other, I on the couch and he in the wing chair. Santos stood off to the other side.

Reilly started, "We're sorry to bother you again, Mr. Hunter. We've been out looking into this matter since we spoke. Talked to the widow, Mrs. Holmes—the deceased's name was Martin Holmes, by the way—does that ring a bell with you?"

When I said it didn't, he continued: "She's quite a woman. She swore on a stack of Bibles that her husband would never have committed suicide. He was very happy. The kids were off to college and doing well. They have a nice home on Big Pine Key. No history of mental illness." Reilly stood up. I hadn't noticed how large a man he was until I was sitting down with him looming over me.

Now it was Santos' turn. "We got a photo of her late husband, and started showing it around town. He did like to go out and catch a drink now and then. Sure enough, we found a couple of people who said they had seen him in the past several days. Seems, in fact, he got into a pretty contentious argument with another guy recently. The description of that other guy generally fits yours. Are you sure you'd never seen or met him before?"

I was getting a weird feeling in the pit of my stomach. "I don't think so. I mean, he was covered in blood . . . and crap. Do you have that photograph with you?"

Santos pulled a headshot, about three by three inches square, from his shirt pocket and pointed it in my direction. I had to lean forward and squint to see it. I almost fell the rest of the way off the couch. It was clearly the asshole who had provoked me three nights before.

"Jesus Christ. Him! Why didn't you tell me!" It was the only thing I could think of saying.

"Why didn't we tell you what, Mr. Hunter? You're the one who told us you'd never seen him before. Are you changing your story now?" It was Reilly again. He was now the bad cop, I could tell. I wasn't even close to saying anything about his badge.

"As I said. I didn't get a good look at him in the car yesterday. The confrontation the other night lasted all of a few minutes. But now that I see his picture, it was him. This is too much. It's a total coincidence." I realized I was sounding a little panicky at this point. Not good. Only the guilty panic. Got to stay calm.

"You're sure it's just a coincidence, Hunter? You sure you didn't get so angry at the guy that you decided to pop him yesterday? That's sure what it looks like to us." Santos again.

"Look you guys. I'm telling you the truth now . . ."

"Oh, so you weren't telling us the truth before?" Reilly interrupted.

"No, that's not what I was saying. I've always told the truth about this whole matter. Yeah, now I realize I met this jerk . . . I mean guy, at Jack's a few nights ago. We got into a little argument. A little one. Nothing major. He was gettin' a little too friendly in my opinion, if you know what I mean." I looked first at Reilly, then at Santos, looking for understanding, but got two steel-cold looks instead. "He came outside as I was leavin.' We had some words. That's all. I don't even own a gun, don't have a criminal record . . ."

"Except for the DUI in Wisconsin, ya' mean. Wasn't that you? Three years ago?" Santos piped in. They were definitely double-teaming me.

"You guys are good. But I was told that'd be handled civilly. I just had to do the program. That's all."

Rusty Hodgdon

Now Reilly: "Also, weren't you stopped by an officer about three weeks ago on Simonton on your way home? Wanted to make sure you were OK? We spoke to him. He said you could barely get your ID out of your wallet. He was going to PC you, but then decided to let you walk the rest of the way. We think you got an alcohol problem."

"That was nothing. I had a few too many. Is that a crime? It's easy here in Key West. Goddamn, every bar has a perpetual happy hour. I'm just not used to it. Yeah, I drink, but not to excess. So does everybody else here."

"Not everybody else gets in an argument, throws some punches, lies about it, and then is caught with a weapon in his hand after the guy is shot. That's your problem now. Tell you what we're gonna do. We can get a warrant if you insist, but we'd like you to cooperate. You're not charged with anything, you're not under arrest. If you cooperate, it'll look good. We want the clothes you wore last night, and we want to send a Special Ops tech over here to do a swipe of your hands and arms for gun powder residue. Will you do that?"

In my past life, I probably would have agreed right away. But I had taken so many hits recently, what with my divorce, I was getting a little gun shy. So I said, "I'm not trying to cause any trouble here, but I think I'd like to talk to a lawyer about this. You guys are making a way too much out of thid. I think it

Suicide

should be obvious to anyone that this guy—what's his name—committed suicide."

With that, Santos suddenly took a step closer to me, his breath reeking of cigarettes. His face was purplish red. He said venomously, "OK Hunter, if that's the way you want to play it. If I have anything to do with it, you're really gonna need a lawyer. Good luck, asshole." They walked out the door.

So much for the good cop. I had this uneasy feeling about both of them. The same feeling a deer must have when the headlights are bearing down on it in the middle of a country road.

SIX

Where do you find a lawyer in a strange town? I knew plenty of them back in Wisconsin. Mostly in real estate. None I would want to represent me if I was in real trouble. The edge of a phone book, which had been collecting dust for a long time under a table in the living room, caught my eye. I guess that's where you start, I realized.

Turning to the yellow pages, I was amazed to see the number of lawyers in this small town. Thinking about it, it was the same all over. Open the phone book anywhere in this country, and the full-page ads scream at you: got a retarded child? Dying of lung cancer? It's got to be someone else's fault, right? We'll get you compensation. Won't cost you a thing. Money, money, easy money.

I just needed some quick advice, and I didn't have a whole lot to pay for it. One small ad caught my eye. It simply read: "Family Lawyer. Divorce, Probate, Personal Injury, Criminal Defense. Honest and Competent." Short and sweet. I liked it. I dialed the number. This early in the morning I only got a recording, so I left my name and number and a request that I get a call back. Good luck, I thought. A lawyer calling me back?

<u>Suicide</u>

I didn't have all year.

I puttered around the apartment for a while trying to collect my thoughts. How could things have changed so dramatically in such a short time? Just twenty-four hours ago I was drifting in a carefree void, or one might say, an alcoholic daze. Now I was the target of a murder investigation. I sat down at the computer, and within minutes, my fingers were flying over the keys. Once again, they couldn't keep up with my thoughts.

This kept up for over two hours, when, promptly at nine, the phone rang. My first thought was, there's Reilly and Santos again. Probably letting me know my front door was about to be broken down as they served the warrant. Instead it was the attorney's office: "Mr. Hunter. Good morning. This is Jayne from Attorney Fitzsimmon's office. I'm responding to your message from this morning. What can we do for you?" Her voice was pleasant, very professional. I was impressed already.

"Well, I was hoping to have a brief word with the attorney. I've got a situation here where I think I should get some advice. Will I be charged if I just speak to him for a few minutes?"

"Let me make a suggestion," Jayne piped in. "Mark—that's Attorney Fitzsimmons's first name—has a policy of giving a one-half hour free consultation on any new matter. Why don't you take advantage of that and speak to him personally? We happen to have an opening this morning. Mark had a case continued late yesterday afternoon. Can you make it at eleven?"

"That's great! Eleven will be perfect. I'll see you then." I got directions, which Jayne gave me clearly and concisely from my place. Now I was really impressed.

SEVEN

The Fitzsimmons Law Office was on Whitehead Street just down from the Court House, as were most of the legal offices in town. I was pleasantly surprised to find it stood alone, not one of those labyrinthine, cookie-cutter complexes that housed multitudinous law offices. Neat, professional gold lettering, with the omnipresent scales of justice on the large window in front, announced the place. I knew the blindfold on Justitia was supposed to signify impartiality—but too many times in my brief contact with the profession, it had meant, at best, myopia, and at worst, a flagrant disregard for the truth.

As I entered, I saw a young lady, about thirty-five, behind the front reception desk, bending over to retrieve a file. She had the shapeliest rear end I'd seen in a long time. I think she knew it, because her tight-fitting skirt perfectly shaped the feature.

She turned, caught the focus of my attention, but only smiled. "You must be Mr. Hunter. I'm Jayne. We spoke on the phone. Why don't you have a seat and Attorney Fitzsimmons will be with you in a minute. Would you like some tea or coffee, or something cold to drink?"

I declined, and took a seat on the comfortable couch that took up most of the space in front of the window. Jayne also had, which I couldn't help admiring, a little pixie face and hair style, set off by very straight, white teeth. She was the personification of cute.

True to Jayne's word, a young man, about the same age as she, came out of a back office. He had a pleasant face, stood about six feet, and obviously stayed in shape. His suit, although not ostentatious, was well-fitted. I, for whatever reason, had expected an older man.

He approached with his hand extended, "Hello, Mr. Hunter. Mark Fitzsimmons. If you don't mind, I'd prefer you call me Mark, if you feel comfortable with that."

"That's good with me," I said. "Please call me Dana."

"Dana it is," he replied with a nice smile. "Why don't you follow me and we'll get started."

He led me into an office behind the reception area. Like his appearance, it was not over-stated, but had a trim, professional ambiance. I felt immediately comfortable in it. There was a medium sized desk and executive chair, with two chairs in front, off slightly to the left. He directed me, however, toward a chair at a small, circular conference table to the right. I noted that in this way I felt equal to him, with no barrier between client and attorney.

Suicide

Mark started by obtaining a brief history from me, after first informing me that anything we discussed was entirely confidential, protected by the attorney-client privilege, and thus I should tell him the complete truth, whether good, bad or ugly. I decided right off I would do just that.

When we got to the events that brought me there, I started with a broad overview, and he decisively honed in on the salient details. As I mentioned my fears about the other guy's sexual orientation, and what I had called him, I thought I detected a vague but fleeting look of distaste on Mark's face. When I referred to the two cops as homicide detectives, he corrected me respectfully. "Actually, Dana, they're technically from the Criminal Investigations Department. Big cities have a homicide division. There just aren't enough murders in the Keys to warrant special treatment. Probably eighty per cent of what they do is drug related. That's the big problem down here. Did you get their names?"

When I told him, I clearly saw a very brief grimace form on his lips, but it quickly passed. "Reilly and Santos are two of the best in the department. Very experienced, very dogged. Some might say a bit overzealous."

"Oh great," I responded. "That's all I need."

"Well, you've got little to worry about, because I believe what you've told me. I say little, instead of none, because the coincidence of circumstances here raises some concerns. My strong advice is that you do not speak with the police again without an attorney present. I also advise that you make them obtain a warrant to gather any evidence. Don't worry about this nonsense of not appearing to be cooperative. It's their job, not yours, to make their case, whatever that might be."

"I think that's good advice," I said. "Would you be willing to represent me at this stage, to get me through this nightmare? And what will it cost?" I really wanted him as my attorney. He definitely knew his stuff, and gave me confidence. That was key.

"I would be pleased to represent you," Mark replied sincerely. "You haven't been charged, and let's assume that will not be the case. So my representation will consist essentially of talking to the police in your stead, and monitoring the progress of the investigation. I think I should also do a little investigating myself. I bill at the rate of $250 per hour, and I would need a $2500 retainer to get started. I will bill against that retainer. Is that acceptable to you?"

It very much was, and I wrote him a check while he dictated a quick fee agreement, which Jayne prepared in less than five minutes, and I signed on the spot.

"Now remember, Dana. You don't talk to anyone, and I mean anyone, about any facet of this matter, except to me. Anybody else can be forced to testify—you're no longer married

Suicide

so the marital privilege would not apply—and you don't need any more misinterpretations or misstatements to cloud this matter. I'll call the detectives now and tell them I'm representing you. Okay?"

My "Yes, that's fantastic" was maybe a little over the top. But when I walked out the door, I felt a hundred per cent better, and believed I was in good hands. That's about the best you can expect from an attorney, I thought.

EIGHT

My good humor lasted about as long as the walk home. By then, I was thinking of the $2500 I was out, just because those two keystone cops couldn't get it right. Of course, I didn't quite make it there. Duval Street beckoned me back. It was already afternoon. A couple of beers couldn't hurt. I had suffered enough already.

By four o'clock, two had turned to twelve, and I missed the call on my cell from Mark. Too much noise in the bar, I guess. I didn't even check my phone when I left at ten that evening. Navigating home took some skill. When I approached my front door, I knew immediately something was wrong. For one, the door was wide open. The second thing was there were two pieces of paper lying on the floor immediately inside the door. I opened the official looking one first, only the booze mitigating the sinking feeling I was getting in my stomach. It was entitled Search Warrant, in large Gothic letters.

The second was a note from Attorney Fitzsimmons, telling me he had tried to reach me earlier to warn me the warrant would be served that afternoon, and that I should try to be there with him when it was. It also admonished me for not staying in

Suicide

contact with him at such a critical time. That really made me feel bad, more for disappointing Mark than having my place searched.

My apartment was a disaster. Not a square inch had been left undisturbed. All the cushions from the couch and chairs were lying in a teetering pile in the center of the living room, my mattress and bedspring, which now lay devoid of sheets or covers, had been pulled off the frame. And, as I soon discovered, every stitch of clothing I owned had been removed. They even got the dirty stuff in the hamper and a wet load from the washer. It was only then that I listened to the message on my phone. It was Mark, essentially covering, before the fact, what I had belatedly discovered in his note.

Man did I have a drinking problem. I laid the mattress on the floor, lay down on it in the clothes I had been wearing all day, and cried myself to sleep.

NINE

Detective Lieutenant Reilly thought he ought to pay another visit on the widow. He knew that women in this situation needed a strong shoulder to lean on. He had to admit, he had been smitten right away. She was a dark beauty—long, black hair with a bronze tint that glowed in the sunshine. Must have reached half-way to her ass. He could only imagine the view from behind when the gentle curls brushed against her mid-back when she was naked.

The thought tantalized him. His separation from his wife of twenty-five years over the past six months had left him almost desperate for sex and companionship. Sure, he had plenty of opportunities. Being a cop offered all kinds of delicious temptations. But he valued his job, and more importantly, his pension, over the siren songs he had heard so far. One of his best friends on the force, Ritchie, had lost it all over one brief fling with an arrestee during a three-week period. Job, retirement, marriage—all gone. That wasn't going to happen to him. He had to be careful. Woo her slowly, cautiously. He knew how to do it.

He could tell she was home when he pulled up in his unmarked Crown Vic. Her car was still in front of the garage, and several lights were on downstairs. Reilly had on his favorite suit—a dark blue pinstripe that fit his tapered torso perfectly.

She answered within seconds after he rang the doorbell. Must have seen me pull up, he mused. She looked more ravishing than he remembered—her hair was pulled up, exposing the delicate nape of her neck—her black dress, a color appropriate for the time, he observed, might have been a touch tight around her hips and derriere. Not that he minded, of course.

"I hope you don't mind me stopping in on you like this," he said. "Just wanted to make sure you were okay. This must be a very difficult time for you."

"Oh Detective, not at all. I really appreciate everything you're doing for me, Martin and the kids." She was all smiles. He hadn't noticed the dimple that graced her left cheek the first time they met. "Please come in," she continued. "Would you like something to drink? I hope you don't mind, but I'm having a splash of wine. It relaxes me when I'm very stressed."

He entered the well-appointed living room where he first had to inform her that her husband had been shot. That's how he had put it. Not being deceptive, for truthfully at that point he wasn't exactly sure what had happened. "Mrs. Holmes, first, I'd prefer that you call me Stephen. Okay? I'm off duty now, and a little wine would be wonderful. If it's no trouble."

"Of course it isn't. And on my part, I'd prefer Jennifer.

Is that alright by you? Just have a seat and I'll be right back."

Reilly nodded his assent to both the question and the assertion. Sitting on the plush couch for a minute, he got up when he noticed an array of family photos on the mantle. There were the usual—one wedding and some pre-kids pictures of Jennifer and Martin, and then the ubiquitous shots of the children, including several family togetherness poses. God, was Jennifer hot, he thought. But he noticed something else. It kind of stood right out at him, in fact. He wasn't an expert at manly attractiveness, really never thought about it. Yet he had to admit that, by any objective standard, Martin Holmes was—ah, had been—an extremely attractive guy. Not in a rough and tumble fashion. Just the opposite. He was almost, well, beautiful. Reilly had lived in Key West long enough to know the look. In each photograph, Martin wore soft tones—light blues, aquas, pinks in two instances. Yes, it could have been the tropical look. But he didn't think so.

Before he could draw any finite conclusions, his attention was diverted by Jennifer's sudden appearance in the room. She was carrying a silver tray with two glasses of red wine and a plate of cheese and crackers. He also noted that she had changed her outfit. The somber clothing was substituted by tiny white shorts and a revealing halter top. Not inappropriate for the temperature of the day and the locale, but maybe for the

Suicide

occasion. He didn't care. She looked sexy as hell. She certainly wasn't into the long-term grieving process. She sat down next to him on the settee.

They made some small talk for the first few minutes—where each of them was from, short histories, what had led them to the present moment. She had grown up in New Jersey, married in college, and raised her family in upstate New York. She and Martin had moved to the Keys—first Largo, then Marathon, on the way to Big Pine—when he decided to retire from his successful design business. Reilly guessed she must have been a good ten years, if not more, younger than her husband.

The detective was more reserved, and normally spoke little about himself. There was a reason for that. His origins were seedier—an unmarried mother, a non-existent father, and a tough street education that finally reaped rewards for him when he was hired—first as a patrolman on the Miami police force for fifteen years, then as a Sergeant, and five years later, a Detective in the Key West Department. In front of Jennifer, however, he felt more open. She was inviting, non-judgmental, and most importantly, he wanted to impress her with his rapid rise through his profession. He opened up to her.

As they spoke, Reilly espied what looked like an envelope, or a sheaf holding some tri-fold pages, on the coffee table in front of them. Jennifer, apparently seeing his focus, picked it up and said softly, "Stephen, I know this isn't your job, but I don't have a man to turn to right now. I found this last night among Martin's financial records. It appears to be an insurance policy. I never knew anything about it. Looks like Martin took it out three months ago. It's for a lot of money. I started reading it, and there's one clause in it that bothers me. I was hoping you'd take a look at it and give me some advice. You run into the law all the time. Maybe you'll understand it." As she spoke, she gently placed her hand on the policeman's thigh.

Reilly pulled the papers out of the holder. There were a lot of them, folded thrice. The name "John Hancock Life Insurance Company" was boldly set out on the outside page, just as the company's namesake had signed it more than two hundred years before. The name Martin Scott Holmes, under the caption "Insured", followed the company designation. Finally came the words and figures: "Face Value ~ Five Million Dollars ($5,000,000)."

"Whew. That is a lot of money!" Reilly exhaled as he spoke.

"Yes it is. And to think he never told me about it. It looks to me he had to put down $50,000, and the annual premiums were $200,000. We don't have that kind of money. But the part I want you to look at is here." Jennifer opened the packet and pointed to a section earmarked with a yellow post-it note.

<u>Suicide</u>

Reilly read the text. The section was entitled "EXCLUSIONS". Under that title it stated:

"The Company shall not be liable to pay over any amounts under this policy if the Insured's death was caused in whole or in part by acts perpetrated by the Insured against himself. This section shall only apply within the first three (3) years of the Policy."

Reilly said, "In my experience, and you should probably consult with an attorney, this is a standard clause in any life insurance policy. Insurance Companies can't afford people taking out policies in anticipation that they're gonna commit suicide. So if it's determined Martin did kill himself, the insurance company wouldn't have to pay."

Jennifer visibly blanched. "Stephen, I don't want to place a burden on you, but I think you should know that, besides this house and a little retirement, Martin didn't leave us with much. I have a little of my own money, but with college costs and everything, it's going to be very tight. When I saw this policy, all I could think about was what kind of life it could bring me, and anybody I might meet and want to spend the rest of my life with." She stifled a sob.

The Detective instinctively put his arm around her. He was a little surprised when she eased into him and let her tears fall on the shoulder of his suit. He didn't mind. Didn't mind at all.

"Jennifer," he said, "the coroner still hasn't issued his report from the autopsy. What we've got now is a suspect who publicly brawled with your husband two days before he died, and then was found with the cause-of-death weapon in his hand within minutes of the shooting. The guy's also a smart-ass. Don't you worry, I think we got the right guy, and it's not your late husband. Leave it to me. This will work out alright."

Jennifer turned her head slightly and gave Reilly a soft kiss on the side of his neck. The feeling was delectable.

TEN

It was another late evening at the Law Office of Mark Fitzsimmons. It came with the territory. There was always something more he could do on his cases. Just returning phone calls took most of the afternoon. Mornings were generally taken up with court matters. The law was a jealous mistress.

He knew he would be lost without Jayne. She was extraordinarily bright, and had worked in the legal field for over fifteen years. Her paralegal degree was only a token of the experience and grace she lent to his office.

Mark poked his head into the secretarial area. "Okay Jayne, time to call it a wrap."

She looked up from her computer with a pleasant smile. "You've got to give me the key for these locks and chains then."

"I'll get it to you when I find it for mine."

As Jayne gathered her things, he asked, "Anything special going on tonight? A hot date maybe?" Jayne's romantic life was always a source of ribald discussion. Being a single woman in Key West, a very sought-after commodity by itself, and her good looks, meant Jayne had a plethora of offers. She was very selective, however, and had recently more or less settled on one guy.

"I'm bushed. Gonna curl up with my book and a cup of hot

chocolate. That's my idea of a hot date. How about you? You and Brad doing anything?"

"No. Just staying home. It's my night to cook dinner. Going to try my hand at some beef stroganoff."

"Oh, too bad. I already have dinner plans," Jayne shot back.

Mark and Brad had been married in Massachusetts two years before. It was truly the only outward manifestation of Mark's homosexuality. He just didn't have any of the affectations that most of his gay friends displayed. Brad was the same. Nor did they adopt any particular roles in their relationship. They were just who they were, and loved each other very much.

Mark didn't mention to Jayne that he also planned to do some investigative work after dinner. He had obtained a snapshot of the deceased in the Hunter case from the police. He could swear that he had seen him somewhere. So he thought he'd show it around at some of the local haunts to see what he could find out about the guy. Mark had developed, as most lawyers have to, a keen sense of when someone was lying to him. He was as sure as he could be that Dana Hunter was telling him the truth. What with Reilly and Santos on the other side, he had to take this case very seriously.

Later that evening Mark and Brad hit Aquarius, 901

Bourbon, and Billy's Monkey Bar, the better-known gay bars. They had no luck at the first two. Nobody acknowledged knowing, or ever having seen Martin Holmes. Finally, at Billy's, the bartender, Michael, motioned them to the end of the bar where things were more private.

"I want this conversation to be confidential. Is that agreed, gentlemen?" Both Mark and Brad nodded their assent.

"I wasn't really shocked when I heard what happened. Martin was living a double life, if you know what I mean." They knew what he meant.

"He and I dated for over a year. Always over at my place. He told me his wife didn't have a clue he was bi. I don't really believe that, because I think most wives are afraid to broach that subject. They know—and I mean *know*—that something's wrong. Martin acknowledged he hated having sex with her, even though I understand she was a real looker. He was very conflicted over his sexuality. Desperately afraid that his wife, his kids, his business associates, would somehow find out. I had to break off the relationship because his depression, his self-loathing became too much to handle. I believe he blew his own brains out. He threatened to kill himself several times in conversations with me."

Mark and Brad had to keep their astonishment under wraps. They asked a few more questions of Michael, got some basic contact information, and thanked him and took their leave.

"I bet you weren't expecting that, were you?" Brad asked of Mark on the way home.

"No, I wasn't. Not to that degree. But something did bother me about Holmes. First, I thought I had seen him before, and since we spend a lot of time in the scene, I figured he might be a part of it. I also believe, as Dana thought, that Holmes was hitting on him at Jacks that night."

"What are you going to do? I'd go straight to the police and tell them what this guy said. If they talk to him, I think they'll back right off. He was very believable."

Mark was used to Brad's naiveté when it came to the law. Brad believed the justice system was designed to exalt integrity and fairness, when Mark knew it actually esteemed the rich and the powerful. He always hated to say anything that would pop Brad's bubble. Nonetheless, he had to be honest.

"I wish, lover, it was that easy. First, remember that we promised that our conversation would be private. Second, I have this suspicion that Michael would be of parts unknown if I ever tried to force him to testify. The guy seems to have some baggage, as do lots of people in Key West, and I don't think he wants much public exposure. Plus, we've got a cop who has a bit of a reputation for being a homophobe. I fear that once Reilly got hold of him, we wouldn't know which story to believe."

"I see what you mean. That's why I don't seek your advice

when doing a shoot."

Mark laughed. Brad was a great photographer, but he'd quickly go broke if Mark had any creative input into his work.

"What did you mean about this Reilly guy? I seem to remember something about him in the news a couple of years ago. He wasn't the one who was accused of planting those drugs on Harvey White, was he?"

"The one and only," Mark replied. "If you'll remember, Harvey was President of the Gay & Lesbian Community Center at the time. As it turned out, Reilly was a fervent Roman Catholic, and a higher-up in the Republican Party here on the Keys. The police raided Harvey's apartment under the pretext of searching for child pornography, and came up with ten packets of heroin. Everyone in town knew that Harvey didn't use, but the cops pushed it to the hilt. Luckily he hired Manny DeRosa, who found a way to expose the whole charade. Reilly was suspended, with pay, for a month. It was laughable."

"Yeah, now I remember. By the way, Manny's the only lawyer I would ever hire besides you."

Not to be bested, Mark shot back: "Well, love of my life, I won't be around if you get into that kind of trouble."

"So seriously, what are you going to do with the information we got tonight?" Brad responded.

"I think I have to proceed very cautiously. Try to get

some corroboration of what Michael told us. Let it out at the right time and in the right doses. I hope I won't have to use it. I think there's still a good chance Dana won't be formally charged. There shouldn't be any gun powder residue on his clothing, and they never swabbed his hands or arms."

Brad had a look of incredulity on his face. "You mean they took all his clothing, but never tested his body? That's unbelievable. What a mistake!"

"I hope that's all it was," Mark said in a somber tone.

ELEVEN

I awoke after a long, sound sleep, with a renewed sense of purpose. It's amazing what a good cry will do. Yes, ladies, face it. Men do cry.

Ate a probiotic yogurt—the stuff really does work—I can testify to it. Had a half cup of coffee. Then went out for a jog. It was still only about 7:30 in the morning. I headed the opposite way to start—toward Southernmost Point. Wasn't ready to return to the scene of the crime quite yet. Threw a towel into my small backpack, and headed off. I was still going strong when I rounded the corner at the Point, and continued on to my ultimate destination—Fort Zachary Taylor State Park.

It was the only decent place to swim in the ocean in the Republic: nice beach, deep water, and no seaweed to speak of. There weren't any tourists at Southernmost at this early hour. Duval was also dead. I loved Duval very early and very late. You got a good sense of what Key West was like seventy or so years ago. When the Master was here writing his great works. Real. Passionate. Classically beautiful.

Taking a quick left at Amelia, I ran at an easy pace to Thomas, and headed north to Southard Street—the entry to the

Park. I still didn't like the idea that you had to pay to get in—who in the heck got that money, anyway?

The ocean was a bit warmer than I would have liked at this time of year, but it was still initially refreshing when I went in. I swam for about an hour. Swimming allows a lot of time for introspection: I had to cut back on my drinking; I also had to control my anger—especially against gays. And I couldn't wait to start writing again.

I ran/walked back to my place. When I returned I suddenly realized I had no clean clothes to change into. I got pissed off again, but, exercising my new way of thinking, calmed down quickly. I left a message on Marks' answering machine to see if he might be able to intercede on my behalf and get some of my clothes back. Realizing that would probably be a long-term project, I hopped in the car—the first time I had driven it in two weeks—and drove to the Key Plaza on North Roosevelt. I'd never been there before—It was the section of Key West I liked the least—but I guess all of Americana had to have its cookie-cutter shopping areas.

I bought some underwear, shorts, T-shirts, and a few tropical shirts. That could be my wardrobe for a month if I needed it to be.

When I returned, I couldn't wait to get back to the computer. But I made myself a sandwich and some coffee, and

Suicide

called each of my kids, leaving a sweet, conciliatory message on their voicemails. I knew I probably wouldn't hear back from them for a week, at least.

Then I started writing. Again, the thoughts came so rapidly I could barely capture them on the screen. I only got up to pee. Darkness settled in and I was still going strong. The floodgates had been opened. Finally.

TWELVE

Reilly went back to the station. It was early enough, but he still had to be careful. As a Detective, even though he could access the evidence room at any time, there was a log in/log out procedure, and since the theft of a kilo of coke four years ago the area was video monitored 24/7. Nodding hello to the night officer, Reilly signed in and punched a time clock, officially sealing the date and time of his entry. Once inside, he went to the pile of four black trash bags holding Hunter's clothing. He pored through them quickly, trying hard to remember exactly what Hunter had been wearing that morning. He was sure it was a white T-shirt. Eventually he located one—it was perfect—still slightly damp and therefore must have come from the load in the washer or from the hamper. Turning his back to the camera—he knew exactly where it was located, because he had helped install the system—Reilly deftly flattened the undershirt under his windbreaker, zipped it up, and signed out.

The Department had built its own firing range in the basement of the station over ten years before. Prior to that, the officers had to use the public range on Long Key, a good twenty minutes away. There was no other available space in Key

Suicide

West, and the residents would never have put up with one anyway. The underground range was small, but fully soundproofed. There were five shooting stations. No one else was around at this hour, as Reilly had planned it. There was no monitoring down here. He chose a station, hit the lights, and activated the target. Spreading his jacket apart slightly at the waist, he fired ten shots in rapid succession, keeping his weapon low at his side and near the undershirt bunched partly under his belt.

He returned to the evidence room, repeating the procedures of his first visit, and carefully returned the article of clothing to the bag. Then he left.

THIRTEEN

Jayne went home to her dark, empty condominium. That was fine with her, though. Not that she didn't like company, or people in general. But after dealing with them all day, often in the worst of their personal crises, she was happy to spend some down time by herself. She also loved her place. It was decorated just the way she liked it. One might call it Key West Idiosyncratic—colorful roosters, geckos, and tropical fish of all sizes and shapes adorned some walls. Local artists' fare graced the rest—quixotic beach and seascapes, mobiles of phantasmal animals, sculptures that required some creative interpretation to identify. But all of it put together in a way that both bombarded the senses, and also soothed the soul.

She checked the messages on her home phone—yes, she still had one. Old habits die hard. Jayne liked knowing there was a back-up to her cell, which she had to keep off most of the day at work. There were also some people she just didn't want to give her cell number to.

There was a message from Paul—the new guy she was dating. Mark didn't know it, but she had met him at the church she now attended on Big Pine Key. It was the only thing that

Suicide

Jayne kept from Mark—her religious beliefs. She had been born and raised a Methodist in her rural Kansas home, had rebelled against it in college at State, and had come full circle back to it here, of all places, in the Keys. Finding a church that would cater to her very progressive version of Christianity was difficult.

So she couldn't believe it when she walked into, purely by chance, a service at the Lower Keys Methodist Church, and immediately felt like she had come home. It wasn't just the message being preached that day—even though she was moved by it. It was the sense of acceptance she felt. It was a fully mixed-race congregation, with at least forty per cent of those present being black or Hispanic. The gay culture was also well represented.

In fact, that's part of what the sermon was about—the love of God forging bonds of brotherhood amongst all peoples. She was mortified whenever she heard the hate in the trill of the Christian right when it came to homosexuality. *I guess God's grace ended with their homophobia*, she thought. She understood implicitly it was because of them that she hesitated in sharing her faith with Mark.

Since they hadn't been able to connect during the day, Paul was just checking in. Jayne called him back, only to get his machine. Then she remembered he was probably playing basketball with the guys. She liked that about him—he was a man's man, but also knew how to woo a lady.

Jayne threw one of her frozen Lean Cuisine's in the microwave, poured herself a glass of pinot noir—she was so impressionable, she thought—she had been drinking that ever since she first saw one of her now all-time favorite movies, "Sideways." With her meal and wine, she settled down to read her book. Jayne would always choose a novel over the tube. Pleasure reading was her favorite pastime.

As her body started to relax, her thoughts, for some reason, wandered to their new client, Dana Hunter. She had instinctively and immediately felt compassion for him. He clearly was desperately lonely, and now was also in deep trouble. She too believed that he had not murdered that man. But she had labored in the legal field long enough to know that justice did not always prevail. She and Mark had discussed the case at length, as they did with most of the difficult matters. He had shared his concerns with her about the two officers leading the investigation, and one in particular. Jayne knew the power the police could exert over the outcome of a case. Mark definitely had an uneasy feeling about the course the case was taking, and Jayne now realized she felt the same. Call it woman's intuition if you want. Something bad was coming down the pike.

FOURTEEN

The next two days were the best I'd had in several years—certainly since my separation. I didn't have a drop to drink. Each of my children called me back well before their usual appointed time, and we had some very meaningful talks. My son wanted some business advice; he had just joined a financial advising firm and was having a problem with a client. My daughter wanted some fatherly advice about her new boyfriend. Altogether I felt closer to them than I had for a long time. Not only that— I was writing like a fiend. And I was pleased with what I was writing. Life was good.

The evening of the second day I was sitting in the living room of my place, reading, when I heard some commotion outside the front door. I half-rose out of my chair when a deep voice shouted "Police! Open the door! Now!" I kept rising, panic stuck in my throat, but before I could even take a step forward, the door literally blew off its hinges. It fell flat directly in front of me with loud whack and a whooshing sound as the air was pushed out in front of it. In an instant, a uniformed cop came barging through the empty space, holding what looked to me like an old-fashioned battering ram.

Rusty Hodgdon

Reilly and Santos popped through next, followed by four more uniforms. Before I could react, I was thrown to the floor, my forehead banging harshly against the ceramic tile, and rudely handcuffed behind my back. Santos yelled, close—a little too close—to my ear, "Dana Hunter. You're under arrest for the murder of Martin Holmes." He then proceeded to read me my rights. I remember shouting that I wanted my attorney present, and Reilly asking me who that was. When I said Mark's name, Reilly said with a sneer: "You are queer bait, Hunter. First you say Holmes was hittin' on you, and now you hire a fag lawyer. Good luck asshole."

I was yanked to a standing position, placed in a cruiser, and transported to the police station. Nothing was said on the way back to the station. Nothing needed to be said. I knew this could be the first day of the rest of my life.

FIFTEEN

The next two days were a total blur. I spent that first night at the police station lock-up. Mark was called and came to see me. He was as surprised as I was, until he heard that the gunpowder residue test—a GRT, as they call it—came back positive on an article of my clothing. We discussed that for a few minutes. The news was so fresh and shocking that we both needed some time to digest it.

I was arraigned the next morning. Mark represented me, appearing for bail purposes only until we could work out the details of the transformed nature of his representation. Bail was set at one million dollars, standard for a first-degree murder charge, or so I was told. Obviously, I didn't make that, and I was transferred, first to the courthouse lock up, and then to the jail on Stock Island.

I reached an all-time low that first night. It wasn't so much the prison. I had anticipated worse. They called it medium security, and I was kept in the protective custody area where they place all new residents for a few weeks to make sure they can get along with the general population. No, it was a combination of the sense of the sheer injustice of the matter, and a stultifying fear that I was in the path of a juggernaut that I had no means to avoid. In essence, it was outraged helplessness. That I was all alone, yet surrounded by hundreds of noisy, discontented men, added to the malaise. Thoughts of suicide crowded my mind. Serious thoughts.

What would drive a man like Martin Holmes, or any person for that matter, to take that final step, to pull the trigger, kick the stool out from under, make that jump? I could only wonder what torment Holmes was feeling that morning. Was it the fear of the ultimate discovery of his bi-sexuality, or homosexuality? That would be the ultimate tragedy in my mind—the biases and prejudices of society could force a man's hand like that. Or was it the conflict in his own constitution? The different sexual drives constantly warring against one another, until only death could bring relief.

As for me, locked up in jail, I don't know what I would have done if I had been afforded the means to escape from the situation via death. I had read someplace that, on average, six people are harshly and adversely affected by someone's suicide. I think some have certainly taken their lives to save themselves, and possibly their family, from the disgrace of a trial and punishment for a crime they actually committed. I knew it would be the horrible impact that my suicide would have on my children that would ultimately prevent me from taking that final step.

Suicide

That coupled with the fact that suicide would have meant no complete exoneration of me in Holmes' death.

Over the next several weeks, I cemented the deal with Mark. No way I was going to lose him now. My best friend from childhood, the only one I had kept up a relationship with, came up with the twenty-thousand-dollar retainer, a real bargain in a homicide case. My kids, who each flew down to visit me in jail, agreed to fund the five to ten thousand for any investigators or experts we might need. That was the hardest part by far—having my children see me in an orange jump suit through a Plexiglas window. To their credit, they remained steady, as if nothing were different, while I wept openly in their presence.

There was no one with the assets sufficient to post bail for me. So, I settled into the prison routine, which consisted of monotony over anything else. For the first two weeks. Mark came to visit me every other day. There wasn't that much to discuss. I filled in more details of my life, how I had luckily been picked off a remote waiting list to attend a prestigious Ivy League college; decided to get into real estate, as my father had, rather than pursue the holy grails of law or medicine as did ninety per cent of my graduating class; married early, had two beautiful children; and then watched my life unravel as the real estate market tanked, as did my marriage.

Mark was still gathering discovery from the prosecution,

which at that point only consisted of the written reports from the day of the shooting, and the GRT results. As to the latter, they claimed there were sufficient amounts of residue on a white T-shirt of mine to confirm that a firearm had been discharged within a foot of it. I knew I was at least twenty feet from the car when the gun first went off, and that was inside a closed car. Mark told me we'd have to hire an expert to re-test the fabric to see if there was a false positive, or possibly the residue was the result of my handling of the weapon. The last was only a remote possibility, according to Mark.

Things did not look good.

SIXTEEN

There were none of the usual dark bags under her eyes in the morning. The dreams of hopelessness were gone, at least for now. Over the past two years or so, as she experienced the reality of living with a man who apparently no longer loved her, Jennifer had the same recurring nightmare. Oh yes, there were variants to the story line. In each one, however, the dominant theme was the same—the sense of unutterable loneliness, the frustration of not being able to extricate herself from the situation.

In one, she was walking on a black sand beach at night time. There were no lights—stars, moon—anything. It was only the sound of the sea that kept her from straying into it and drowning. There was not a single, living soul around. She had to get off that beach, toward some light, some human sight, sound and touch. But the sand was soft and mushy, and as she pushed forward with each step, it almost felt as if she were losing ground. Over and over she fought forward, trying to make progress, but to no avail.

In another, she was in a crowded theater. But crowded wasn't the word for it. The hundreds, possibly thousands of people around her, were packed together, shoulder to shoulder, back to back, front to front. She could not move, raise an arm, take a step. So tight she could barely breathe. She tried to talk to the people around her, find out what was going on, see if they could move apart, even a little. But either they could, or chose, not to answer her. Instead, they, each one of them, kept up a loud, indecipherable moaning. She knew she was going to suffocate and die, all alone, no one knowing why, or caring.

Yet, fantastically, after Martin's death, the dreams had suddenly stopped. Instead, she slept soundly all night, sometimes as many as eight or nine hours, never cognizant she had any dreams at all, even if there were some. Although she would never admit it to anyone, she knew why. Her marriage to Martin—shaky from the beginning—had turned into a living nightmare, which, of course, translated into the sleeping kind.

She had sensed from the start that something was amiss. He just didn't seem to have the same drive as other men, sexual, economic, you name it. She was able to overlook that, primarily because of his movie-star good looks, and also his money. He had inherited a handy fortune from his father, who died while they were courting. Jennifer had visions of leading the kind of life she could only have imagined before—world travel, fine restaurants, blessed repose.

But none of it was to come to fruition. Immediately after

Suicide

the wedding, Martin took total control of their finances. She had to beg for enough money to pay the bills. They never went out, never traveled. Martin, however, took numerous so-called "business" trips, staying away sometimes for weeks. His explanation of his whereabouts was always very hazy, the details never coming into focus.

So it was not a complete surprise when Martin announced to her, at the time she had asked for a new car, her 1998 Toyota on its last legs, that there was no more money left. Thank God she had insisted that he fund college accounts for the children. Throughout it all, there had been persistent rumors of heavy gambling, and prostitutes, the sex of whom was sometimes an issue. After the money ran out, and Martin could no longer disguise his exploits with geographical distance, the scuttlebutt focused on local liaisons, again of questionable gender. They themselves had not had relations for several years. Jennifer had decided long ago to ignore the talk and do the best she could to raise the children alone.

That's exactly why she now felt so attracted to Detective Reilly. He was everything her husband was not—strong, manly, decisive. Basically, he had his full measure of testosterone. Girls, when your man don't have that, you don't know what you're missing. And Jennifer knew she had been missing a lot. She trusted that Stephen would follow through with his promise. She

<u>Rusty Hodgdon</u>

also felt intuitively that he would do anything to accomplish a goal he sought after.

SEVENTEEN

Returning home from a visit with Dana, Mark was in a particularly bad mood. After forcing himself to present an upbeat persona in front of his client, he allowed himself some down time upon his exit. He had nothing new to report to Dana in over three weeks, and his own investigation was stalling. It was nice to arrive back at the house and find Brad knee-deep in a veal marsala he was preparing for dinner.

"Hey there, lover-man," Mark said as he walked into the kitchen. "How's it goin'?" Brad's hands were covered with the dough that would ultimately become the Italian bread to accompany the meal, so they just gave each other a light peck on the lips.

"Actually, had a great day. Finally got that Webster shoot done. What a chore that was. But now on to bigger and better things."

Mark knew the project Brad was referring to. It had been on both their minds for weeks now. Brad was one of the top photographers in the Keys. To make decent money, though, like most he had to cover the commercial work. This was an ad for a well-known women's cosmetics company, and the model they had foisted on Brad had been impossible. Sara Webster was an American princess of the nth degree, and seemed to delight in not showing up, or showing up late, and demanding the most spurious of amenities before she would allow a single shot to be taken.

"That's great! Now when does the check arrive?" Mark joked.

"Ah, the most important part," Brad added.

Mark went upstairs, showered and changed. At dinner, they covered the rest of their respective days. Then, invariably, the talk turned, as it too often did, to the Hunter case.

"How'd the meeting with Dana go?" Brad opened.

"Okay. Not a lot to talk about at this stage. I did get Tommy on it."

Brad recognized the name. Tommy Gleason was the only gumshoe Mark would ever use. He was totally out there, but honest to a fault. And relentless. If there was something to be discovered, Tommy would find it.

"I told Dana that I was making arrangements to get down to the station with our expert to look at the T-shirt where they say they found the gunpowder. Dana confirmed that, to the best of his memory, he was wearing a white undershirt that morning. Of course, he didn't know which one. The cops offered to return the rest of his clothing, but I felt it best to leave it there. Can't say why. Just a feeling, I guess. Anyway, Dana won't need it where he is."

"What is Tommy doing?" Brad inquired.

"I've got him trying to track down Michael—you remember, the bartender who spoke to us that night and knew a lot about Martin Holmes. Apparently, Michael took off—literally—left his job and the apartment he was sharing. His boss says he thinks he may have returned to New England to be closer to his family. Didn't have an address or a phone number, so Tommy's poking around to see if he can locate him or anyone else who has some knowledge of Holmes."

Brad's downcast demeanor reflected this news. "That's not good. I thought what Michael had to say was invaluable to the case. Do you think you'll be able to find him?"

"It was very important," Mark responded. "I have no idea, unfortunately. Even if we did, it would be tough to get him to return here if he was reluctant. I might be able to get a court order, but I'd need some cooperation from him. Also, an angry witness is sometimes worse than no witness at all."

"So where do you go from here?"

"Just keep moving forward. See what Tommy shakes up. Get our expert to test the clothing. Wait for something to pop."

"I hope for Dana's sake something does," Brad said glumly.

EIGHTEEN

Reilly had decided to wait a week to call. Couldn't sound over-anxious, ya' know. So he was pleasantly surprised when he saw her number pop up on his cell caller ID. Her message was soft and sweet. Would he be able to stop by sometime soon? She had a few more questions about the case. He felt the rise in his crotch area when he thought of her. Certainly, he'd be able to stop by. Professional courtesy.

They agreed on eight o'clock that evening. That left enough time for him to go home, shower, and change clothes. He thought about a uniform this time—he still had one available, and knew women went gaga over them—but decided on another suit. All of them were tailor made, and would be equally impressive. What would she wear, he ruminated? It would define how she felt about him. He was certain she was attracted to him. Very few women were not.

His question was quickly answered as soon as she opened the door for him. She was in a white chemise that fit tightly around her ample breasts and hips. Her naturally dark brown skin tone was accentuated by the color. Her thin, supple thighs were nicely exposed beneath the short dress. The entire presentation broadcast sensuality. Reilly could barely stay upright.

"Jennifer. You look radiant this evening," was all he could get out.

"You don't look so bad yourself, Detective."

He sensed she used his title rather than his first name as a measure of respect, but also endearment.

"Please come in. I really appreciate you stopping by."

"My pleasure, entirely," he replied.

She led him into the living room, where she had already set out a plate of small sandwiches adjacent to two open bottles of wine, one a Pinot Grigio, the other a Merlot. Kenny G was lightly playing in the background.

"I couldn't remember if you liked red or white, Stephen. I forget what we had last time so I brought both. Would you like a glass?"

So she was back to his first name. That was good. "That'd be great. I'll take the red, if that's OK."

"Of course, Stephen. I think men should drink red wine, don't you? White's a little effeminate."

"Well, scotch is my drink. But yeah, I agree. When I see a guy drinking white wine, it makes me wonder. Especially around here," Reilly said, doing a sweeping motion with his arm toward the town in general.

"Oh, Scotch. I'm sorry. I didn't know. I'll make sure I

have some next time." Jennifer distinctly winked at him as she said, "next time."

"Not to worry. Just being here with you is all the narcotic I need." With that, he firmly grasped her hand. She did not flinch at all, but in fact, accepted his hand fully. Hers was delicate and small.

They engaged in some small talk. The funeral had come and gone since they had last met. Reilly had attended, but had not spoken to Jennifer except to briefly extend his regrets. Of course, she knew through reading the paper that someone had been arrested for the killing after the residue had been discovered on his clothing. Reilly had also called her immediately after the arrest to inform her, but they had only discussed the matter quickly. This was their first real opportunity to catch up.

Jennifer began. "You've made an arrest. That's fantastic. It just all seems so crazy, that this complete stranger would walk up and shoot my husband in the head. In broad daylight, out in the open, so to speak. I can't believe it."

"I've been in homicide for over five years now, and the one thing I can tell you, there's rarely any rhyme or reason to cold-blooded murder. It's always more than is necessary. But humans are killers. That's how we worked up to our present place on the food chain—on top." Reilly picked up one of the sandwiches and popped it into his mouth.

Suicide

"I know you're right, but I'm already worried how this is going to sell to a jury. What about the gun? Do you know where that came from?"

"Yes, it was apparently bought from a gun dealer, at one of those fairs they hold, in South Carolina about ten years ago. The buyer was a Glen Frieze, who lived down here for a while. He died of natural causes two years ago. We figure Hunter must have purchased it on the black market when he got down here. You can buy anything in the Keys, as you know." He winked at her.

"Well, I've only heard about that, as you can imagine." She smiled softly. "Do you think the fact that this Hunter fellow has been identified as the person my husband quarreled with, was holding the gun shortly after my husband was shot, and had the residue on him, will be enough to convict him?"

"I think it should be," Reilly said. "Of course, it's always better to have more evidence. Amazing what these defense attorneys can do. We're still investigating, and hope to dig up more."

"The reason I'm concerned is that I did meet with an attorney. You know, about my husband's estate, the insurance, and all. He told me it's likely the insurance company will not pay until they see how the trial comes out on Hunter. If he's found not guilty, I'd really have to fight to get the money. He also told me there was another clause in the policy. Double indemnity I think he called it. Apparently if it's shown my husband was killed, that's considered an accidental death under the policy, and they have to pay twice the face amount on the policy. Do you know what having ten million dollars would do for me and my family, Stephen? It would change everything. It's something I could then share with the next man in my life."

"Ten million is a lot. That's great Jennifer. Well, all I can tell you is, as the lead investigator on the case, there's no way Hunter's gonna' fall out of my web."

"Thank you, Stephen. I know you'll do your best. I so appreciate all you've done already." With that, Jennifer gave his hand, which was still on hers, a gentle squeeze.

As Reilly was leaving, Jennifer gave him a hug. They lingered together for a few seconds. Reilly drank in the smell of her perfume and body. As he got into his car, he thought, *gotta' close the noose around this guy tighter.*

NINETEEN

Usually, all visitors to the jail had to meet the inmates in the general visitation area, which consisted of a bank of stalls along three walls facing inward, each containing a chair and a telephone. The inmates came through a door in the fourth wall, and would sit across from the stall. A two-inch thick Plexiglas shield separated them from their visitor. Obviously, there could be no contact.

Jayne passed through the metal detector and showed her paralegal certificate and letter from Attorney Mark Fitzsimmons to the guard. The letter announced that Jayne was there on official business as part of the legal team. Usually only the actual attorney of record could gain such access, but the guard relented and showed her into one of the small rooms that were designed for attorney-client conferences. The fact that Jayne was wearing one of her tight little skirts and tops didn't hurt matters.

The "official business" part was a half-truth. Mark did want her to talk to Dana to fill in some minor gaps in his history. But the real reason, in Jayne's mind at least, was that she felt a lot of empathy for Dana. She was part of the prison visitation group sponsored by her church, so she had been to the jail on numerous occasions. She knew the loneliness and abject despair most inmates felt. A friendly face and voice, follow-up letters and cards, could make an incredible difference in a prisoner's life.

If she was really truthful, however—and she was—she had always had a thing for older men. It started when she was twenty-one and fell for a judge she had met during one of the many court appearances she had attended with Mark. He was incredibly good-looking—in a craggy sort of way. He was at least twenty years older than she. He also had that judicial bearing that made him appear wiser than he could possibly be. She always wondered to herself—and not openly to anyone else—if the reason for her attraction was that her father had died when she was only ten, and she would forever seek men who would supplant that awful void in her life.

Nothing ever happened with the judge—Dan was his name—because she wouldn't let it. Not that he was without interest. It became a tad embarrassing when he would search her out at bar association functions she attended with Mark. Jayne was imbued with a moral sense that belied these times. Dan's wife had died in a car accident five years before, leaving him with five younger children. Jayne did not want to create complications for them.

She expected the look of surprise on Dana's face when he entered the room. She knew this room was where he had previously met with Mark at least a half-dozen times. She also did not fail to notice when the surprise changed quickly to pleasure.

"Hi Jayne, I didn't expect to find you here. Is Mark OK?"

"Oh yes. He just wanted me to go over some things with you. He thought you wouldn't mind. You don't do you?"

"Not at all. Heck, you're a lot prettier than he is anyway."

This evoked a pleasant smile from Jayne. She couldn't help but notice that Dana had lost some weight since she had last seen him several weeks ago. He also looked more fatigued—dark circles underscored his eyes. Yet, he was still very attractive.

"How have they been treating you here?" Jayne asked.

"I can't complain. The food is worse than bad, but I needed to lose some pounds anyway. No one has bothered me. I pretty much keep to myself. It's very lonely though. But I have the use of the library computer for an hour and a half a day so I can type up what I've handwritten. I'm still writing every day."

"That's great. Do you need anything—paper, pens, pencils? I'd love to read it when you've finished."

"No, thanks. We're quite limited in what we can have here. My children brought me everything else I need. I'd definitely like your feedback on the writing. I think this first one is going to be a short story. Would like to limit it to under a hundred pages. Work up to a full-fledged novel."

"That sounds like a good plan. If you ever do need anything, though, please let me know. I'd like to help."

"Jayne, just your being here is help enough. Knowing that someone cares means the world to me."

"It's really not a problem for me. I only live about three miles away. Takes me under ten minutes to get here. I'll come as often as you like. Hopefully we can keep meeting in this room. It's so much better than the visitation area."

"You can say that again. Seeing my kids there really sucked. Couldn't give them a hug or anything. That was very difficult having them see me like this . . . in this place." Dana's voice cracked slightly.

"I understand. I have complete faith that Mark's going to get you out of here. I can't say when, but he will. I just feel it."

"Thanks for the optimism Jayne. I believe he will too. I'll be patient. Nothing I can do about it right now anyway."

"Well, guess we ought to get down to the "official business" part of this. Wouldn't want to have lied to the guards," Jayne said with a grin.

She started to go over some of the areas Mark had asked her to inquire about. Just a little more detail. Although Jayne had to admit to herself that her interest in them was a bit more than "official". She already knew that Dana was divorced with two grown children, and had pursued a career in real estate. She learned today that he graduated from Princeton Summa Cum Laude in English literature. He had wanted to, and did, teach for several years at a local high school. But his early marriage and arrival of children forced him to pursue a more lucrative occupation. The market was booming at that time. His father had been a broker all his life, so Dana pursued real estate. Except for sublimating his creativity, it worked well for him.

During the conversation, Jayne found herself opening up to Dana. Except, of course, about her attraction to older men. She had been married—once before—and very briefly. They had been too young, and penniless. She had moved to Key West on a lark after the divorce. Had originally, like so many before her, planned to stay a week. That week became twelve years. She would like to remarry, but just hadn't met the right guy yet. She neglected, with some guilt, to mention Paul's name.

Their conversation flowed easily, such that their allotted time of one hour seemingly passed by in a few minutes. When they said their goodbye's, Dana thanked Jayne profusely. She promised to come back soon. They gave each other a hug—at first haltingly—but then comfortably as their bodies and arms seemed to meld effortlessly. Jayne became aware for the first time of Dana's scent. Was it Old Spice, that her father used? Whatever it was, it created a pleasant nostalgia of him. Not disagreeable

Rusty Hodgdon

in the least.

TWENTY

Doggedness was certainly one of his better qualities, Tommy thought. He had known Mark for over fifteen years, worked for him for ten. During that time, he had advised Mark on several occasions to give up the ghost on certain investigations. Mark refused, even though Tommy's rationales for the recommendations were sound. In two cases—and Tommy remembered them well—Mark's persistence paid off. Big time.

The most famous one was when Mark insisted they continue looking in the landfill for a gun their client said he heard had been disposed of by the real killer. If it was there, and had the other suspect's finger prints on it, their client would be vindicated. After two straight days of digging in the smelliest garbage you could imagine, in the middle of a Florida summer, to boot—and despite Tommy's continuous protestations—the gun was found. The problem was it had been carefully wiped clean of prints, but ultimately was connected to the other guy sufficiently that their guy walked.

That's why Tommy was not surprised when, on this Friday night when they were out asking around about anyone who might have run into Holmes, Mark grabbed his arm at two AM and pulled him to the next bar. They had already learned from the owner of the establishment where Michael had worked that Michael's disappearance coincided with a visit to him by the cops.

"C'mon, this is the best time to talk to people," Mark explained to Tommy. "The gay scene doesn't get hot until after one o'clock. And at this hour, most will have had enough to talk freely."

"But we've hit eight places already. I've been at it since six this morning. Let's give this a rest, at least until tomorrow night," the investigator complained.

"Yeah? What were you doing that early in the morning. Strubbin Sally, I bet."

"Well . . . maybe," Tommy confessed. "But it still takes a lot of energy."

"Tell you what. We'll try Aquarius, then 901 Bourbon again. If nothing pops at those two places, we'll head home. Deal?"

"OK. You're the boss. But I get time and a half after midnight."

"Sure you do. Just like me," Mark replied while giving Tommy a soft tap on his large bicep.

Nothing happened at Aquarius. The night club was in the middle of its late night drag show, so it was hard to engage anyone. Nobody recognized Holmes' photo, or at least wouldn't admit they did. 901 was much quieter. The upstairs late show was over. The downstairs Saloon was crowded, but the music was at a reasonable volume. There was more leather than at a tack shop, Mark mused. Great get-ups—one guy had on a black leather vest and short-shorts with a chain-mail belt. Another displayed skin tight purple leather pants with only crisscrossing leather straps and large silver buckles adorning his upper body. It wasn't Mark's style, but anything went in the Conch Republic.

Here, Tommy and Mark were a little more circumspect when they approached the patrons. They ordered sodas and chatted with the bartender. After about five minutes, another man sat two stools down from them and appeared interested in the discussion.

He eventually introduced himself as Steven Weeks, and added, "I couldn't help but overhear you about that murder, or whatever it was. I never met this guy Holmes, but I'm a freelance photographer, and do some work for the Key West Voice. I keep the police scanner on all the time, and on that day, I got over to the scene within a few minutes of the cops arriving. I only live three blocks from there. One of my photographs appeared on the front page of the Citizen. I don't know if you saw it, but it was the close-up of the driver's window of the car, and you can easily make out the victim's bloodied face through the hole in the glass. Took some effort to get that one."

"Did you take any other shots of the scene?" Mark inquired. "Any of the defendant, Mr. Hunter?"

"Yes, I took quite a few. I think I may have included him in one or two."

"Do you think I could see all of them. I'd be willing to pay you."

"I don't see why not. I'll tell you what. It's easy for me to make copies. If you give me your card, I'll send you a full set. Would a buck a photo be fair?"

"More than fair," Mark said as he handed Steven his business card. "When do you think you can get them to me?"

"I'll mail 'em out tomorrow. No problem," Steven responded.

"By the way," Mark inquired. Did you tell the cops about these pictures?"

"No. I didn't think they were that important. Why?"

"Well. If you don't mind, I'd like to keep them just between us for now. OK?"

Steven gave Mark a conspiratorial look. "No problemo. Just between us."

The three men engaged in some light chit-chat for a few minutes, and soon Mark and Tommy took their leave. On the way down Duval, as they looked for a cab, Tommy asked: "Why'd you

Suicide

ask for the pictures? The police gave us over twenty, of every angle of the scene. I doubt that guy's will be very helpful."

"Well, for one, the photos given to us by the prosecution do not include a single take of Dana at, or around the scene. Only his mugshot, which is cropped just below the neck. I don't know exactly why I asked for them. Just a nagging suspicion that something was missing from the discovery documents given to us. Call it a gut feeling. That's all."

"That's good enough for me", Tommy said. "Let me know when you get them. Two of us looking might be better than one."

They grabbed two cabs. Tommy lived on Stock Island over near the hospital, and Mark on Rose near Leon. Mark promised to give Tommy a call the next day.

TWENTY-ONE

Benny Hopkins was nervous. If you asked anyone, they'd say he was naturally the most nervous person they had ever met. He fidgeted constantly. Ran in twenty different directions at one time. No wonder he was chronically unemployed and now homeless.

He spent most of his time on Duval weaving cock-eyed baskets out of green palm fronds. Occasionally a tourist would buy one, more out of a sense of mercy than want. Maybe they'd go home and tell their friends that they had bought an original work from a Conch native. Then the damn things would begin to stink after two weeks as the palm began to rot.

When he wasn't on Duval, Benny would spend his time wandering the streets of Key West, getting down to the beach to sleep and bathe, trying to find a quiet area at night where the cops couldn't find him. This particular night he was heading down to the youth hostel on South Street. The hostel was the *de facto* shelter of the town. He had met a guy on the street who said he could get him some blow. Cheap. The arrangement was that Benny was supposed to meet him at the hostel. Then they'd go down the street to a quiet corner and do the exchange. Benny had a rare twenty in his pocket that an older lady had given him that day for two baskets. He had worked her good. Telling her how he had lost his wife and two children in a terrible car accident three years previous. Of course, it was all a total lie.

The guy he was supposed to meet was standing at the corner of Vernon and South, just west of the hostel. Benny's stomach was churning. A bag of raw nerves. He had done time for dope related offenses, and didn't want to go back in. But he needed some stuff so bad he was willing to take the chance.

"Hey, Benzedrine," the guy yelled from across the street. That's what everyone called Benny. He hated it, but couldn't do anything about it. Benny headed toward him.

"Ya got the cash, Benzedrine? Don't come near me if ya don't."

"I got it, I got it," Benny stammered.

"Okay, follow me then," and the guy headed south on Vernon. Benny did as he said. Scared out of his wits, because the guy was large and very tough looking. He could get ripped off. Beaten up. Go to jail. But the siren song of the dope kept him going.

When the guy took a left onto Waddell, Benny hesitated. This was a very poorly lit area with run-down homes and older commercial buildings.

"C'mon Benzedrine," the guy yelled. "What the fuck ya

doin? Do ya want your blow or not?" Benny followed. As they approached the intersection of Waddell and William Street, the man stopped and turned to face Benny. Benny slowly walked up to him, oblivious to the fact that the front doors to a dark gray Crown Vic were opening just around the corner.

"OK, here's your money," Benny said as he extended the twenty out to the dealer. "Now give me the fuckin' blow." Benny thought by sounding tough he might not get the shit kicked out of him.

The guy held out a small square, folded scrap of tin foil. Just as Benny reached for it, two burly men in suits raced around the edge of the building at the corner, grabbed him and threw him to the ground.

"Gettin' a little sugar tonight, huh Benny?" one of the men said derisively as he placed his knee firmly in the square of Benny's back. Benny was cuffed and rudely dragged across the sidewalk and thrown into the car. The other suit yelled back over his shoulder, "Thanks Jack. We'll return the favor." The guy gave a quick wave and disappeared down the street.

Benny was blubbering now. He got one "Help!" out through the partially open rear passenger window, and was promptly rebuffed by a sharp slap across his face by the man in the front passenger side.

"Shut up, Benzedrine. You do that again and I'll break

Suicide

your nose." Benny stayed silent. They drove for about five minutes to an empty, vacant lot near one of the Navy compounds that dot the island. Benny peed himself. The non-driver, who was the largest of the two, turned to their passenger: "Benny, do you know who we are?"

"No . . ." Benny stuttered. "I don't think so."

The man gave him another hard slap, emitting a sharp cracking sound within the interior of the vehicle. Benny let out a low moaning sound, and began whimpering.

The man held up the tin foil packet and said, "I'm Detective Reilly, and this is Detective Santos. Key West Police Department. And tonight, we're your worst nightmare. Do you know how long you're gonna cool your heels in prison for this one Benny? Years, especially with your priors. You're fucked."

Benny couldn't say anything he was so scared. The whimpering continued. Until the cop gave him another whack, this time alongside his head.

"Please don't hit me again. Please!" Benny wailed.

Now the driver spoke. "But Benny. You know we have some heart left. It doesn't make us feel good to send you to jail for most of the rest of your life. Maybe you could help us out, and help yourself as well. What d'ya think?"

Benny lifted his head as if he suddenly saw a ray of light from the heavens. "Ahh, what you mean by help?"

"Well listen carefully, cause I'm only going to go through this once. Understand?" Benny nodded his head affirmatively.

"Did ya read about that murder over on South Roosevelt a few weeks ago? Guy was shot in the head in his car."

"Yeah, I heard about that one," Benny mumbled.

"Well we know you spend a lot of time right near where he was killed. On Smather's Beach. Don't you?"

"Yeah . . . I guess so."

"Well, we know you happened to be sleeping right on the other side of the sea wall when the shooting happened. Isn't that right?"

"Nah, I wasn't anywhere near there then," Benny protested.

Another slap across his face, this one harder. It almost fulfilled the Detective's promise to break his nose. Benny screamed in pain.

"You're not getting it Benny," the other Detective continued. "You were sleeping there, and got woken up when you heard loud voices. Two men arguing. Weren't you Benny?"

"I . . . I guess so." Benny was now getting the drift of things.

"That a boy, Benny. And when you heard the arguing, you peeked over the edge of the wall. That's when you saw this man," and the cop shoved a photo of Dana Hunter under his nose. "You saw this man pull out a gun, open the passenger door, and fire at the driver. Right?"

"Oh, am I gonna get in more trouble for this?" Benny lamented.

The passenger side cop raised his hand again, but did not strike. Benny involuntarily flinched.

"The only trouble you're going to get in is with us. Now, listen carefully. Here's a police report of the incident. You're going to sit here and read it. As many times as necessary so you've memorized every detail. And we're going to test you on it. You're not leaving this car until that's done. Then you're coming to the station. Tomorrow at ten. Tell the officer at the front that you have important information on the Holmes' case. Got that? Holmes. Say you need to speak with someone. He'll take you to our office. And there you're gonna give us a full statement about what you saw. Any questions so far?"

"No. I guess not." Benny had plenty, but he wasn't going to ask them here. Not now.

"We're gonna keep this coke. If you do as we say, meet with us, and stick to your story, and testify in court if necessary, then nobody will ever know about our little episode tonight. You got that?"

Benny nodded again. The two men showed him the report, and sat while he read it over several times. Then they grilled him on it: descriptions of the participants, of the car, of the words that were spoken. Telling him he didn't come forward until now because he was too frightened. When they had finished, Benny, even in his diminished capacity, had his story down pat. They removed the handcuffs and let Benny out of the car.

"Remember Benny. Tomorrow at ten. Be there or be square," the passenger cop said sarcastically. Benny just nodded his head again as he scurried away out of the lot.

TWENTY-TWO

The package arrived at the office just two days after Mark and Tommy had met the photographer. True to his word, Steven had blown up thirty photographs of the shooting scene. They were color glossies, sandwiched in between protective cardboard sheets. A bill for thirty dollars accompanied the packet. Jayne had opened the mail that morning as she always did, and had the shots spread across her desk when Mark arrived.

"Hey, what's that," Mark asked as he approached her area.

"The photos you asked that guy to send to you. They're pretty good quality."

Mark looked over her shoulder as Jayne went through them one by one. Plenty of shots of the vehicle, from every conceivable angle—the partially open passenger door—the jagged hole in the driver's window. One in which you could just make out the gruesome head and face of Martin Holmes.

The rest were of the entire scene—the numerous police cars, ambulances, the surroundings in which the incident occurred, the condominium complex across the street, the thick concrete wall separating the road from Smather's Beach and the ocean.

There were only two of Dana. In the first, he was seated in the back of an unmarked police car. One could barely make out his upper torso and face. In the other, he was out of the car, the handcuffs were off, and he seemed to be in the middle of a gesticulation while talking to Reilly and Santos—his right hand, chest high, pointing toward them, his left low, the index finger also extended, as if he were trying to make a strong point in a debate. The detectives had a quasi-bemused look on their faces. This photo was quite clear and detailed. Dana was wearing his jogging clothes—sneakers, low cut white socks, dark blue shorts and white T-shirt. The cops were in their obligatory dark suits.

"Darn, I was hoping there'd be more of Dana, showing his demeanor, his expressions at the scene. Anything," Mark said wistfully.

"I agree," Jayne replied. "I don't see how this helps much. There's nothing of the interior of the car. I was wishing for something there. To see if there was any glass in the compartment to show a bullet could have come from the other side."

"Well, Tommy and I will spend some time on them with a magnifying glass. There's got to be something in there that can help us. Tommy's good with that. He often sees things that totally escape me."

"That's a great idea. By the way, have you been down to

the station to look at the things they took from Dana's apartment?" Jayne asked.

"Not yet. Our expert on the powder stains is supposed to call me with some dates he can come down and test the shirt. I'll take a look at the rest of the clothing then."

"Sounds like a plan," Jayne responded. "Do you mind if I come with you? Maybe the female perspective will add an element to the investigation. There's something nagging at me. Maybe something Dana said to me. I just don't know. I would just like to see the clothing. OK?"

"You got it babe," Mark replied. "How's our boy doing, by the way?" Mark was aware that Jayne had been to see him several times. He encouraged it.

"As well as can be expected. I think he puts up a strong front with me. We've written several times. He's an excellent, sensitive writer. He wants me to retrieve his laptop from his apartment and read his recent work. Do you think that's OK?"

"I don't see any problem with it. Frankly I'm surprised the police didn't take it."

"Me too," said Jayne.

Mark went into his office and began doing work on some neglected cases. Jayne continued to examine the photographs carefully.

TWENTY-THREE

The paper was a torn sheet from a spiral note pad, the envelope standard government issue. But Jayne didn't care. It was the content of the letter that had wowed her.

It was kind of nice corresponding by paper letter, Jayne thought. It seemed it had been a long time since she had done that. Oh, she was good at getting cards out with short messages. For birthdays, holidays, anniversaries, etc. But really communicating with someone? Sharing her innermost thoughts? *Too long, that's for sure,* Jayne acknowledged.

It was the third letter she had received from Dana. She had sent him two. She decided to read it again as she sat out on her porch. The native parakeets were chattering loudly away in the palms. A gentle early October breeze coaxed her skin. It read:

My Dearest Jayne:

You have no idea how much I appreciate you! You are truly an angel from the heavens! I'm not so sure I could survive in here without your visits and epistles. Guess I've gotten too dependent on them!

I'm sure you have clients, accused of committing crimes, that insist all the time in

Suicide

their innocence. And many times you have seen the evidence mount up against them until there is little doubt of their guilt. But I only had to tell you once that I did not commit this crime. And not once have you wavered in your belief that I spoke the truth. I so appreciate that!

You began to tell me about your faith in God during our last visit. And I think you certainly understood that the little faith I may once have had has long been extinguished. Yet I must admit I am considering re-visiting that faith. And that is because I see in you the purest form of spirit: non-judgmental, loving, sensitive, caring for others. If only there were more like you! Then I think the world would see the essence of Christianity, what Jesus really stood for: loving others above all else, with no regard for requitement, for reciprocity, in that love.

Well I ramble on. I just wanted to share some of my true feelings with you. Don't be scared! I could accept our relationship just the way it is for eternity. But if there is to be more, I await it with bated breath.

With all sincerity,
Dana

She set the letter down on the wicker table in front of her . . . and brushed a small, rolling tear from her cheek. She had certainly been in love with several different men in her lifetime. But Dana had struck a chord in her that no one else had strummed.

Jayne decided to respond at once while her emotions were

still fresh. Dangerous, but worth it.

> Dear Dana:
>
> Thank you for your beautifully written letter. I also appreciate the compliments, even though I don't think I deserve them . . . well, maybe some! I know I have enjoyed our relationship as much, if not more than you. Although I am not in a physical prison, I think all of us can work ourselves into emotional incarceration, and not even realize it until someone comes along and unlocks the barred gate. Frankly, I now realize that's where I've been for some time – locked up without a key. You have offered me a way out.
>
> I also say: don't be frightened. If this is all there is to be, so be it. But I do envision more.
>
> I'll come to visit you soon, definitely in the next several days.
>
> Love,
> Jayne

Jayne also realized she had to do something about Paul. He was starting to show signs that things were getting serious on his end. She needed to let him know right away that he should back off. She hated any confrontations, but she could not be deceptive about her feelings for him. Best do it now rather than labor over it. Jayne went to the phone, called Paul, and was honest with him. He took it OK, but she knew by the end of the conversation that he still harbored strong hopes that he could win

Suicide

her over.

    Isn't this always how it goes, Jayne mused to herself. Three months ago I had no one. Now I have to brush someone off to leave things open with another.

TWENTY-FOUR

Jennifer just happened to be admiring the colorful bouquet in the light blue vase on her dining room table when the phone rang. From the caller ID she could see it was Stephen.

"Hi there. How are you?" she said as sweetly as she could.

"Doing well. Especially now that I'm talking to you. How about yourself?" Detective Reilly responded.

"Very well. The flowers are exquisite! Thank you so much. You really shouldn't have."

"The least I could do for the most beautiful lady in the land."

"Stephen. You're so romantic. I love it."

"Hey. There's a major break in the case. Would it be all right if I stopped by to tell you about it. I'm right in the area."

"That would be fantastic. Can you give me fifteen minutes?"

"I can give you all the time you want, honey. Fifteen it is. See ya' soon."

Jennifer went into whirlwind mode. Re-applied her make-up, brushed her hair, and changed into a sexy outfit, all in the span of ten minutes. Amazing what a girl can do when she's

Suicide

motivated, she thought to herself.

He arrived in exactly fifteen minutes. Looking dashing as usual. This time a light green, summer weight suit, with a yellow button-down shirt and light blue tie. A matching paisley handkerchief in the pocket rounded out the ensemble.

On her end, it was light blue, very short shorts, exposing her slender, well-tanned legs and thighs. A pink, low-cut blouse offered a tantalizing glimpse of her ivory colored Victoria Secret embroidered bra and ample cleavage.

They exchanged pecks on the check, and she led him by the hand to the couch.

"So what's the new news, Stephen. Is it good?"

"It's very good. After a great deal of investigation—I mean scores of hours knocking on doors, going into restaurants and bars—we found an eyewitness. He was afraid to come forward at first. I can't say he's an ideal citizen, but his recollection is excellent.

He says he was just on the other side of the seawall, fishing, when the incident took place. He heard some arguing, so he peeked over the wall. That's when he saw Hunter take aim and shoot your husband at point blank range. No question in his mind about what he saw. He was so frightened of the gun he ducked back behind the wall and stayed there until everyone had left. He knows he should have come forward and spoken to the police, but it all happened so fast, he was in shock. He's ready to testify now, though."

Jennifer showed real shock. "I can't believe this. This is fantastic. Hunter can't get away now, can he? With this, the insurance company can't say Martin committed suicide, right?"

"Well, Honey. You know nothing's certain in life. But this really cements the case against Hunter, in my opinion. I think we're looking a lot prettier than we did yesterday."

"Do you think this new guy will make a good witness?"

"I think he'll be OK. We'll prepare him well. And I can tell you, he's motivated."

"Stephen, I can't thank you enough for all you're doing. Oh, what a bad hostess I am. Can't I get you anything? Something to drink. To eat?"

"Well, Jennifer. There is something you can give me," Reilly said as he moved closer to her on the couch and took her hand. "I've been so lonely. I haven't dated since my separation, months ago. Just didn't want to get into it. I'm so attracted to you." He placed his other hand on her thigh just above the knee. "I think we're ready to move this to the next level. What do you think?"

Jennifer was anticipating this, but knew when to play coy. "Stephen, you know I'm very attracted to you too. But wouldn't that just complicate things? I mean we have to work together on the case. I imagine I'll have to be a witness. You know I want to, but is it the right time?" She placed her hand on the top of his on her thigh, and in doing so, moved it slightly closer to her crotch.

Reilly breathed deeply of her perfume, a hint of musk hanging in the air. Her hair was a rich black, not a hint of gray, shiny and healthy looking. Desire was overcoming him. His erection was pushing hard against his pants.

He reached and pulled her head toward his. "I know it's the right time. Please Jennifer. I need you. Now." He kissed her, the tip of his tongue exploring gently around her lips. Her breath was minty, but hot.

She kissed him back. Tentatively at first, then opening her mouth fully to take in his inquisitive tongue. Low moaning sounds emitted from his lips. Primordial. Atavistic sounds.

They were kissing deeper and deeper now, their lips and cheeks wet with each other's saliva. Reilly reached around for the back of her bra, and when he could not get the clasp right away, pulled down hard. The gossamer fabric ripped away easily.

"Oh Stephen," Jennifer whispered.

He was on top of her now, pulling her pants down with one hand. She resisted slightly, but then relented, moving her hips to facilitate the removal of her shorts and panties. He reached down, undid his zipper, and pulled out his throbbing cock. It was enormous.

She gasped when she saw it. "Oh, be gentle, Stephen. Please!"

There was no gentility in the way that he took her. He thrust his hard penis abruptly into her wet pussy, driving it to the hilt in the very first encounter. Jennifer let out a yelp. He was in a frenzy now, pumping forcefully against her hips, gyrating. She gave it back as best she could, but this was his show. She sensed he needed total release.

Soon he did that, yelling "God! Fuck!" as he came deeply inside her.

She could actually feel the spurt of the hot semen against her vaginal wall. They lay on the couch, with him still inside her, for minutes. Exhausted. Spent.

Slowly Stephen got up, withdrawing from her in the process. He pulled his fly up. He was still fully clothed. "That was the best, baby. But I gotta' go. I'll call ya' soon."

With that he walked out the door.

TWENTY-FIVE

Sometimes good luck comes in tandem. Sometimes it lands in your lap. Other times you have to work for it. It came to Mark both ways, now eight weeks since Dana's arrest.

The first was a letter from Michael. He had been reading about the case on the internet. Felt bad for Dana. Thought he was probably innocent, and felt it was his duty to testify as to what he knew about Martin Holmes. How he led a double life. And was clearly suicidal. If he flew down for the trial, assuming there would be one, could Mark guarantee his safety?

He also expressed to Mark why he had suddenly taken off. He had been paid a visit by two plain clothes cops at the bar. It was late. They let him know in no uncertain terms what "could" happen if he didn't get out of town. Michael had a record, albeit minor stuff. Two convictions for possession of some small amounts of coke, and some petty larceny raps. But just enough so the gendarmes could make his life mighty uncomfortable if they wanted to. So he took off and went home. Michael included his contact information.

Mark called him right away, had a nice chat, and was convinced that he would return for the trial if Mark paid for his ticket and lodging. As for his security, Mark said his private investigator had a couple of friends who would be glad, at Mark's expense, to attach themselves to Michael for the duration of his visit. Even the cops wouldn't tangle with these guys.

The second took some work. Mark had just received the supplemental police report detailing the prosecution's uncovering of an eyewitness to the event. It also contained a summary of the witness' expected testimony, and the guy's full name and address.

Mark called Tommy and read him the report. Tommy said he had an idea, and Mark gave him the go-ahead.

Tommy found the address was the hostel. A quick check revealed that "Benzedrine" Benny, a/k/a Benjamin Hopkins, and various and sundry other appellations, had stayed there on and off for a few days over the past several months, but was not a regular resident. Tommy located Benny's regular spot on Duval, where he created his palm frond masterpieces.

Tommy went to the liquor store and bought a half-pint of Jack. He then nonchalantly walked past Benny late one weekday night and stopped, ostensibly to admire his handiwork. Tommy then feigned that he had spent his last nickel on some booze but he wanted the small purse Benny had fabricated and displayed on the sidewalk. You know, as a present for his girlfriend. Needed something to patch over some differences they had that day.

Suicide

Instead of cash, how about the bottle Tommy had on him as payment. Benny was more than happy to oblige.

Tommy returned two hours later to buy something else. His significant other liked the item so much he wanted another trinket to take back. This time he had cash. So Tommy picked up a crappy little bracelet, paid the few bucks, then suggested that Benny join him for a drink at the Green Parrot around the corner. On Tommy. In thanks for helping him make things right with the little lady back home. Benny, already half in the bag, could not believe his good fortune, and jumped at the chance.

By three o'clock the next morning, Benny was so drunk Tommy had to peel him off the bar stool. Not coincidentally, a car was parked, engine running, just down on Whitehead Street. In it were the two guys slated to look after Michael when he came down. This was also the part Tommy chose not to tell Mark about, and Mark didn't care to ask.

Tommy brought Benny out, holding him under the arms, and walked by the car. As if on cue, the two men jumped out and threw Benny into the vehicle. One stayed in the back seat holding him down, while the other sped off. Tommy kept walking down the street and went home. He had a professional license to lose, so what was going to happen next was none of his business.

Benny, whining and protesting the whole way, was taken to a non-descript trailer sitting on a lonely lot on Sugarloaf Key.

A rolled up and knotted wet towel can be a very effective truth serum. The beauty of it is that it works, but leaves no scars. The two men worked on Benny, who was now gagged and tied to a chair, for about a half hour, until they could tell from his stifled screams that he was ready to tell them anything they needed to know.

When the gag was removed, he did just that. For a guy like Benny, the immediate pain was the motivator, not what might happen afterward. A tape recorder picked up the whole story. They, of course, first had Benny state unequivocally, while the machine was running, that he knew he was being recorded, and assented to it.

They let Benny sleep it off, after giving him copious amounts of aspirin, and stuck him on the Greyhound to Miami with fifty bucks in his pocket, not failing to tell him what would happen to him if he ever returned.

Sometimes you just gotta fight fire with fire.

TWENTY-SIX

Remarkably, the guards were still allowing Jayne to use the attorney's room when she came to visit Dana. She guessed it was more an indication of the respect they had for Mark. But she also confessed it might be due in some part to her feminine wiles, which she was not adverse to exercising where needed. She never knew who was hornier—the inmates or the guards.

Prior to coming to the jail for her visit, and with Dana's encouragement, Jayne had retrieved his laptop from his apartment. Dana had given her the password to access his writings. The first was the beginning of the short story he had talked about: the strange goings on in a town in California. She enjoyed the thirty or so pages that had been completed, but also felt that the prose was a bit heavy, and certainly noticed the anger that subliminally arose from the text.

She was surprised to find a second story that immediately followed that first one. Dana had not mentioned this work. It too was around thirty pages long, but a completed tale. In somewhat autobiographical form, the story was essentially about an older man who had lost his wife to cancer, and fell in love with one of the young nurses he had befriended during his long vigils at his wife's bedside. Now the prose was light and upbeat. It was also the most beautifully written love story Jayne had ever read. Her tears would have wet the pages if it had been in paper form. And she knew instinctively it revealed Dana's feelings about her. A man who wrote so sensitively about love must be able to give love in equal measure, she surmised.

On this particular day, Dana appeared especially optimistic. Mark had communicated the good news to him—at least an abbreviated version of it. This time the peck on the cheek got noticeably closer to the mouth.

Jayne did have some official business. She had drafted an outline of the direct examination Mark could use if he decided to put Dana on the stand. Of course, it was Dana's ultimate decision. But so far Mark had established such a rapport with him that he had no doubt Dana would heed his advice on the issue. So she intended to run Dana through the outline to prepare for his testimony, if needed. They didn't get very far on it. Dana wanted to discuss other matters.

"Jayne, isn't it great about those two witnesses, Michael and Benny? Seems Michael's really on our side, and will come through for us. Benny, of course worries me. He's really unpredictable. Are you sure he won't come back and still testify he saw me shoot Holmes?"

"Nothing's certain, honey, but Tommy tells me he was able

to show Benny the error of his ways. He doesn't think we'll ever hear from him again. But in a way, it doesn't matter. Mark thinks he could decimate him on the stand if it got that far. Almost to the point where it'd be better if he did show up."

Dana did not fail to notice the "honey" thrown into the mix. That alone thrilled him more than the good news they were discussing.

"Does Mark have to reveal Michael's existence to the prosecution?"

"Yes, but not what he'll testify to. They can try to talk to him, but Michael says he has no interest in doing so. I think he can avoid them because he's not down here to take any heat."

"Looks like the pieces are starting to fall into place. Do you think it's possible the prosecution will drop the charges? I know that sounds like wishful thinking, but Jayne, I can't wait to see you under normal circumstances. Like over a nice dinner at the Grand."

"I can't wait for that either, Dana. Hold it. Are you asking me out on a date?"

"Well, take it as you will. Sure sounds like it to me," Dana said.

"I'll tell you whether I accept or not when we get your butt out of here."

"I can live with that, cutie-pie."

They both had a nice laugh over that exchange.

Jayne continued: "But more seriously. I don't think, and you'll also have to ask Mark on this one, that they'll drop the charges so long as they have the gunpowder evidence. That's critical. We have our expert testing the clothing day after tomorrow. We should know more then. Let's keep our spirits up. As you said, things seem to be going our way. But you never know when God will throw a zinger in your path."

"Yeah," Dana replied. "Like that old guy in the Bible. What was his name?"

"Do you mean Job?"

"Yeah, that's the guy. Wasn't he really devoted and faithful to God? Then God made him go through all these horrible experiences. What was with that?"

"Well, as they say. God works in mysterious ways. I'm no Bible scholar, but I think God sure made his point to the Devil. Despite all the hardships Job had to endure, he came out of it with a stronger faith than ever. I guess that's the message. We can never get discouraged to the point where we give up. Because God will always see us through to the end."

"That's a nice way to look at it. Does that guarantee this trial I'm facing will turn out okay?" Dana said a bit tongue-in-cheek.

"Only if you have faith, my love. Only if you have faith."

Suicide

The guard motioned that their time was up. For the first time they gave each other a light brush across the lips. For Dana, it was the most beautiful thing that had happened to him in years.

TWENTY-SEVEN

She finally summoned the courage to call him. It had been two days since he had come over and done what he did to her. Jennifer's emotions were highly conflicted.

She was extraordinarily attracted to him. He was so masculine, so tough. The roughness of the sex, and his cavalier attitude afterward were certainly part of those characteristics. But they also signaled something else. An intrinsic meanness? Even cruelty? She could not believe the man she had come to know, even love? To whom she had bared her soul, could be a monster. She had been harboring fantasies of spending the rest of her life with him. Now she was not so sure.

He was not at the station when she called, but he returned her call within minutes. He explained he was actively involved in the investigation of Martin's death right at that moment, but again, happened to be in the area. Could he stop by just to talk? Fear at first grasped her by the throat, but with it also came an excitement over the prospect of seeing him. She said yes.

When he arrived, he looked as dapper as ever. She had never seen him in the same suit twice. God was he handsome! She melded into his arms when he came through the door.

Suicide

"Stephen, why haven't you called me? It's been two days."

Reilly appeared visibly irritated. "Jennifer, as I told you, I've been up to my ears in snakes with this investigation. Now our eyewitness has disappeared."

"You mean Benny? Disappeared? What happened?"

"Just what I said. He's been a fixture on Duval Street for years. And well-known to the police as well. He never goes anywhere. Now no one knows where he is. Of course, he could be holed up someplace. It's only been a few days. But it is strange."

"What does that mean for the case?" Jennifer asked with some panic evident in her voice.

"Nothing, cause we're gonna find him. I'll guarantee you that. He couldn't be that far away. The guy had no money, and would hardly be the type you'd pick up hitchhiking. I'm sure he's somewhere in the Keys."

"OK. As long as you're not worried, I'm not worried. But I am more concerned about us, Stephen. I'm not sure you have the same feelings for me that I have for you."

"Jennifer, you're wrong. Look, I know I can be a bit rough with the sex. And a little insensitive. The job makes me that way. I can't help it. I'm extremely attracted to you. But you have to accept me the way I am."

"Oh, I want to, Stephen. I really do."

"I'm not sure you have a choice, honey. I'm the one person

who can make your dreams come true. Without me, I don't think you have a prayer of getting that insurance money. I've already done whatever it takes to make that happen."

"I know you've worked very hard on the case Stephen, and I really appreciate that. I just need to know that it's not only sex and the money. That's not all there is, is it?"

"Let me show you what it is Jennifer." He picked her up in his arms and carried her upstairs to the bedroom. Jennifer protested meekly, but he ignored it. He undressed her roughly, ripping her blouse in the process. This time he removed all of his clothing. Jennifer gasped when she again saw the massive size of his penis.

He took her in every position imaginable. Missionary. From behind. Her on top. Culminating in an explosive ejaculation.

This time they lay together for a while. Jennifer was hurting, but had never before experienced such pleasure.

"That was fantastic, baby," Jennifer said as she stroked a line down the center of his chest with her finger. "You are huge. And a great lover. If that's all it's going to be, I guess I can live with that."

"That . . . and the money, honey. Let's not forget about the money. Great combination in my book."

"Yes it is. And who knows, maybe, just maybe, we'll fall in love in the process. That would be sweet."

"I wouldn't hold my breath, sweetheart."

Again, Reilly got up, dressed quickly, and left, merely saying, "See ya later," as he left. No kiss. No hug. Nothing.

TWENTY-EIGHT

Mark met his expert, Walter Haller, at the Police Station. Haller had brought all the equipment necessary to test fabric for gunpowder residue. It was contained in two large trunks that were stacked in the reception area when Mark entered. Jayne had driven separately, and came in right behind him.

Mark was now in a high state of alert. The news of Benny's recantation, and the pressure placed upon him by Reilly and Santos, had confirmed his worst fears. Could it be that all the rumors regarding those guys could be true? And what did that mean for his defense of this case? Like most, Mark needed to "get along" in his profession. There were certain things you just had to overlook. But this was not one of them. Strangely he wished it weren't true, that he could attack Benny just like he would any prosecution witness: his ability to perceive, the incredulity of the perceptions he had. But Benny's story of what the Detectives did to him raised the bar on this defense. Mark knew he was in very dangerous waters. Sharks abounded. He went into the testing of the shirt with grave misgivings.

"Hey Walter, how's it going?" Mark had known Walter for over ten years, and had used him several times, as well as seen him in action on the stand in other cases. He was utilized by the prosecution and defense alike, a testament to his unbiased expertise. It was also fortunate he resided in Miami Beach, only a three-hour drive, or half hour flight from Key West.

"Doing well, Mark. You look great. How do you stay so in shape?" Mark did notice that Walter had added a few pounds since he had last seen him.

"It's the stress of the job. That's all. Would keep anyone from eating well," Mark quipped.

Mark introduced Jayne, and the three of them proceeded into a small conference room set aside by the Chief for them to do their business. The clothes taken from Dana's apartment, as Mark had requested, were still in trash bags and stacked in a corner of the room.

Walter began unpacking and setting up his equipment: an expensive looking microscope, several test kits, vials, and a professional camera. As he worked, Jayne asked how he was going to go about his testing. Sensing she had little knowledge of the process, and always eager to pontificate on his favorite subject, Walter explained, "The first step is to visually and microscopically examine the evidence, in this case the T-shirt. The presence of any gunshot residues found on the fabric will be documented."

The police had set aside the T-shirt that had been tested by their expert in a single, sealed, clear plastic bag. Walter removed the seal, took the shirt out with gloved hands, and turning it over and over, examined it carefully with his naked eye. He then began sliding the fabric under the lens of his microscope as he observed.

"There's definitely residue on this article of clothing," he said quietly to Mark and Jayne. "In fact, a great deal more than I would have expected, considering there was only one shot fired. That's right, isn't it Mark? One shot?"

Mark nodded his assent.

Walter continued his recitation as he proceeded, "The next two steps involve chemically processing the exhibit for gunshot residues. The first chemical test conducted is called the *Modified Griess Test*. This test is performed first on the exhibit because it will not interfere with later tests for lead residues. It's a test to detect the presence of nitrite residues. Nitrite residues are a by-product of the combustion of smokeless gunpowder. When a firearm is discharged, nitrite particles are expelled from its muzzle and firing chamber and can be embedded in or deposited on the surface of a target or the shooter."

Walter pulled some supplies, including some colored paper and chemical vials, from a box. He also removed a standard iron from a bag and plugged it in. Jayne, anxious to break the tension with the realization that the presence of gunpowder on Dana's clothing was probably going to be substantiated, said: "I guess I

<u>Suicide</u>

should have brought my laundry."

Walter smiled weakly, and began dabbing the paper with several solutions as he spoke. "This test is performed by first treating a piece of desensitized photographic paper with a chemical mixture of sulfonic acid in distilled water and alpha-naphthol in methanol. Desensitized photographic paper is obtained by exposing the paper to a hypo solution. The photographic paper will no longer be light-sensitive but will be reactive to the presence of nitrite residues."

Picking up the now hot iron, the expert continued with his running narrative. "Now the back of the exhibit being examined is steam ironed with a dilute acetic acid solution in the iron instead of water. The acetic acid vapors will penetrate the exhibit and a reaction takes place between any nitrite residues on the exhibit and the chemicals contained in the photographic paper. The resulting reaction will appear as orange specks on the piece of photographic paper."

Indeed, as he ironed the shirt, muted reddish-orange dots showed up almost magically on the paper.

"The last test conducted on the exhibit is called the *Sodium Rhodizonate Test*. This chemical test is designed to determine if lead residues are present on the exhibit. It's performed by spraying the exhibit with a weak solution of a mixture of Sodium Rhodizonate and distilled water. This solution has a dark yellowish/orange color. The exhibit is then sprayed with a buffer solution which causes the background color to disappear. The Sodium Rhodizonate reacts with any lead that may be present and turns the lead a very bright pink. The pink color is only an indication of the presence of lead residue.

"To confirm the presence of lead residue the area must be treated with a diluted Hydrochloric Acid solution. If the pink turns to a blue, then the presence of lead is confirmed."

After using a plastic bottle to spray the shirt, the three of them gathered around the T-shirt. Sure enough, spots of unusually bright pink slowly evolved before their worried eyes. Walter sprayed another chemical on the same area, and inexorably the pink turned to a light blue.

Nothing was said in the room for a few seconds. Finally, Mark spoke: "I guess there's no doubt that Dana fired a gun while he was wearing this shirt. Is that right Walter?"

"No doubt. The only other explanation is that someone, wearing the same shirt, discharged a weapon either before or after Dana went out that morning. Which we all know is highly unlikely."

Jayne was unusually quiet. Mark noticed she was fixated on the shirt. The silence in the room became almost embarrassing.

"What's up, Jayne? Is something bothering you?" Mark

finally asked.

"Mark, you're about Dana's size. Here, put on the shirt." It was more of a command than a request. Jayne was in a heightened state of agitation.

Walter cut in. "I'm not so sure you should do that. The state may claim you tampered with the evidence."

"Fuck the state!" Jayne exclaimed. Now she was really out of character.

Mark did as he was told. He removed his suit coat, tie, and shirt, and pulled the undershirt on. He then stood there with an expectant look on his face. "Now what, Jayne?"

"There's something wrong here. See, this is a regular T-shirt. The sleeves come down about four inches and cover the top of the bicep."

"So?" both Mark and Walter said, almost in unison.

"Those sleeves would cover any tattoos on the upper arm. I'm sure I could make out a tattoo on Dana's arm in the photographs we got from that guy. Do you have them with you, Mark?"

"Yeah. I brought the whole file." Mark opened his briefcase and pulled out a thick file. Fingering through it, he located the sub-folder with the pictures and spread them on the conference table in front of them. All three of them leaned over and carefully studied the ones showing Dana.

"Yeah, here it is," Walter first spoke. He was pointing to the shot of Dana standing and talking to the two plainclothes cops. His finger rested on what, with the naked eye, appeared to be a black smudge on the upper part of Dana's right arm.

"Let me get my glass." Walter came prepared. He rustled around in one of his satchels for a few seconds, and came up with a very substantial looking magnifying glass. Again, the three of them gathered around the photo while Walter placed the glass over the spot.

"Holy Jesus!" Mark shouted first. "Not only can you easily see the tat, but look, the sleeves on the T-shirt Dana was wearing that day appear to be cut off."

Sure enough, the glass detailed the ragged edges of a shirt whose sleeves had been scissored, and not delicately, so that most of the upper arm was exposed. There was no doubt about it. The shirt in the photo was not the same one still being worn by Mark and stained with gunpowder.

TWENTY-NINE

The silence in the police conference room was more prolonged than the one that had followed their initial conclusion that the shirt had gunpowder residue on it. Mark, Jayne and Walter were simply stunned with the realization. Mark broke it in a whisper. "I don't know if we're being listened to right now, so no one say a word. Not a word." He pulled off the T-shirt and Jayne helped him replace it in the plastic bag, making sure the permanent evidence stickers were firmly affixed.

"I've got an additional idea," Walter suggested in a low voice. "Let me do a quick visual of all of the other undershirts in the bags, including the cut-off one. We don't have time to perform full tests on them, but at least I'll be able to say we examined them by eye."

They each took a bag and carefully looked through it. To their surprise, there was no shirt with the sleeves trimmed off. Luckily there were only five other white T-shirts. Walter scrutinized each carefully, both with his naked eye and then with his magnifying glass. He concluded there was no trace of residue whatsoever on any of the fabric.

After placing the shirts back in the bags, Walter packed

up his equipment. The three walked out of the station without speaking.

In the parking lot, and out of earshot of any eavesdroppers, Mark said in a low voice, "Walter, thanks so much. Don't forget to send me a bill. Include an advance for your testimony if you want. But remember, not a word of this to anyone. And I mean anyone."

Walter nodded his head in the affirmative. He was a professional, through and through.

Mark and Jayne drove back to the office in their separate cars, both deep in thought. The treachery that underlay the discovery was disturbing. When at the office, Mark called Jayne into his. There was no one else around.

"I don't know what to say," Mark began. "I mean, this is great for Dana. My first thought is, I think I may be able to get the charges dismissed. But I'm also very concerned that we didn't find the shirt he was wearing that day. I mean, where in the heck is it?"

"I was thinking and asking myself the same things," Jayne added.

"But we have to be careful with this," Mark continued. "Very careful. Someone went to great effort to contaminate that shirt. We've now got multiple witnesses to the fact that the T-shirt in the evidence bag is not the one Dana had on when Holmes shot himself. I don't want whoever did this to get wind of our discovery and locate the cut-off shirt and do whatever he did to get the residue on that one. And toss out this one."

"You got that right," Jayne responded. "I didn't think of this, but is it possible that the cut-off, where ever that might be, has residue on it as well? Maybe the two were packed against each other in the hamper, or somewhere else in Dana's apartment."

"That's an interesting thought," Mark said. "Let me see if I can reach Walter on his cell."

Mark dialed Walter from the office phone and punched the speaker phone button so Jayne could listen in. "Hi Walter. Are you alone?"

"Yup. On my way back to the office to write up my report on the findings made back at the station. I was going to include my conclusions with the other shirts as well, unless you don't want me to."

"Hold off on reducing anything to writing right now Walter. You can jot down some personal notes, but no official report. Ultimately, I'd have to give that to the State Attorney. I want to avoid that as long as possible."

"I understand," Walter said.

"I've got one more question for you, though, if you don't mind."

"Of course, I don't mind. Shoot."

"Is it possible that the shirt Dana wore on the day of the killing had gunpowder on it—from the shooting—and it somehow came off and tainted the shirt we examined? I mean, what if both shirts were in the same load of laundry or something—right next to each other. Is that possible?"

Walter thought for a few seconds before answering. "It's hard to say that something's not possible. There are just too many random scenarios out there. What I would say is that it's highly unlikely. In fact, extremely improbable, to use more legal terms. First, there's just too much residue on the subject shirt. Contact alone with other stained fabric would not do that. Second, the residue is literally seared into the fabric of our test clothing. That occurs as a result of the heat from the combustion of the gunpowder. That, of course, could not occur with mere proximity to another article of clothing. I think we're safe in saying that the residue on the test piece had to come from the firing of a weapon. How that happened, I hate to think."

"I do too, Walter, I do too. Thanks so much for all your help. I'll be in touch."

Mark turned to Jayne after hanging up. "We've got to tell Dana about what happened today, and try to jog his memory on what he might have done with the shirt. Let's make arrangements to see him as soon as possible, OK?"

<u>Suicide</u>

"Absolutely," Jayne agreed.

Mark saw now that things might get bad. He just didn't know quite how bad.

THIRTY

He was beside himself. Reilly had been forced to pull a lot of favors. Cops up and down the Keys—even as far north as Homestead—were on the look for Benny. But the reports were not good. There was simply no sign of him. He had strangely vanished. He didn't believe Benny had the wherewithal to get to Miami on his own. If he somehow did, the Detective knew he didn't have a rat's ass chance of finding him. The City was a haven for drifters, misfits, and outright crooks. Benny could easily disappear there if he wanted to.

But who had gotten to him? Reilly was sure Benny didn't take off on his own. There had to be a greater threat than Reilly posed. Which had to be substantial. If Reilly did find him, the only thing that would keep Benny alive would be his value as a witness, as badly compromised as that might be now.

That wasn't the only bad news. The assistant State Attorney had called him the day before to announce that Fitzsimmons had revealed the existence of a new witness for the defense. According to the report, this guy was going to say that Martin Holmes led a double life—dutiful father and husband at home—queer poacher away. Worse, the witness alleged that

Suicide

Holmes had spoken of taking his own life because of the charade he had lived for years. On more than one occasion.

Reilly was a man of action. He took on life like he took women. Hard. Forcefully. He sensed Fitzsimmons had something to do with Benny disappearing. He had to find a way to back him off. To let him know it wouldn't be a cakewalk from this point on.

THIRTY-ONE

She and Mark were going to see Dana tomorrow. It was not information they could impart any other way than in person. She was excited over the prospect of seeing him, of giving him the good news. They both agreed they had to be careful now. Someone was trying to set Dana up, for whatever reason. And that person couldn't be too unfamiliar with the police station. It was great having the police on your side when you were in trouble. It was terrible when they were working against you. They largely held the cards.

It had been early to bed tonight. The events of the past few days had been exhausting. Jayne gently dozed off.
She smelled him first. At least that's what she thought. It was an odd combination of men's cologne and sweat. She knew the former well—an old boyfriend had used it. Then she became visibly and audibly aware of the presence of someone in her bedroom—a slight wisp of motion, of sound over on the side. She froze, but did not panic. Her daddy had taught her that one too.

He had also taught her how to shoot. And where best to keep a gun handy. And as her daddy always told her: "You don't need .357 magnum—but when you do need one—you really need

Suicide

one." Her fingers slipped quietly to the crack between the mattress and box springs on her side of the bed. The intruder, thankfully was on the other.

She found the trigger guard of her weapon and was able to get her hand around the grip just as the intruder began to reach for her arms. She instinctively swung first. Always time to shoot later. The hardened steel weapon caught him—and she knew it was a he by the low, guttural sound of the grunt—full bore on the jaw.

He backed off for just a second, but with the light of the outside street lamps filtering through her French blinds, she could see him coming again. Now it was time to pull the trigger. Which she did. Three times in rapid succession. Took all of a quarter of a second. Each round blew the man backward, up against the side wall, where he slithered into a heap on the floor.

After the emergency personnel, cops and techs had left, she learned his name was Ronald Gaston. Had been bounced out of the force in Key Largo ten years before. Tried to get a disability pension, but no one would buy it. There was no traumatic stress syndrome as he claimed. The fact was, Ronald was bad to the bone. He had drifted in and out of criminal behavior ever since. Mostly petty larcenies. A few strong-arm deals. Minor drug offenses. Nothing as serious as a B & E night time, with intent to . . . one could only guess. But as Mark learned, he was a guy who had the reputation that he'd do anything for hire.

Mark took the initiative on this one. Paid to put Jayne up at the Crowne Plaza for a week while the professional cleaners did a thorough mop-up and a high-tech security system was installed at Jayne's apartment, all at Mark's expense. Given the circumstances, there was this overwhelming feeling that the attack was somehow connected to Dana's case. He even hired Tommy and his cohorts to provide 24/7 protection for Jayne while she was at the hotel.

First Benny. Then the T-shirt. Now an ex-cop. Mark now realized exactly what he was up against. At least he thought he did.

THIRTY-TWO

Over Mark's vehement protestations, Jayne insisted on carrying through with the plan to see Dana that next morning. There would be a coroner's inquest over the death, of course, but the outcome was a *fait accompli*. They had found a glass pane in the back door, expertly cut out to give access to the lock. Gaston wore gloves in the Key West heat. His record belied any legitimate intent for being in Jayne's apartment at two-thirty in the morning.

Jayne was rattled, but determined. Dana was being framed and nothing was going to deter her from helping uncover it. She also didn't want Mark to back off out of fear for her safety. They had a lot to tell Dana.

They were able to get through security at the jail with relative ease. However, their wait in the attorney's room dragged on. Dana simply did not appear. Jayne grew apprehensive. Finally, Mark started to make some noise with the nearby guards, and the Deputy Superintendent suddenly appeared. He looked embarrassed.

"I understand you're here to see Dana Hunter. I can't believe they didn't tell you at the main gate. We had a little incident here early this morning."

"What kind of 'little incident'," Jayne almost shouted. She stared at the man with piercing eyes.

"Settle down, now," he said sternly. "Mr. Hunter is going to be all right. But we had to transfer him to the Lower Keys Medical Center on Stock Island for further testing. He got into a fight with another inmate. No one else was present, so we have two very conflicting stories. I'm afraid there might have to be some disciplinary action taken as well."

Jayne would not be that easily quieted. Mark decided to sit back and let her take the initiative.

"First of all, Mister . . . I'm sorry, I didn't catch your name."

"Mr. Sullivan, Deputy Superintendent of this facility. And to whom am I speaking?"

"You're talking to Mark Fitzsimmons, Mr. Hunter's attorney," Jayne said, nodding in the direction of Mark, whose smug expression hinted at the fact he found Jayne's aggressiveness entertaining. "I'm Jayne Curlette, his paralegal." She was now right in Sullivan's face. He appeared intimidated, as if he had never been spoken to by a woman like this.

"We need to know what happened, and we need to know right now. I was attacked last night by a complete stranger in my own home, and we have no doubt this attack on Mr. Hunter was orchestrated as part of the same plot."

"Well, I don't know anything about those matters," he said, almost stuttering over his words.

"No you don't, but you will. First, we need a full incident report on the assault against Mr. Hunter, and second, we need to speak with him. Immediately!"

"I'm not sure a report has been prepared yet. And I'm sorry, we don't have adequate staffing at the Hospital to allow you to see Mr. Hunter."

Mark now entered the fray. He was heated as well. "Mr. Sullivan. In one minute, we're walking out of here. At which time my first call is going to be to Judge Smoot, the First Justice of the Circuit Court. That will be to arrange an emergency hearing before him this morning for an injunction requiring you, and your staff, to allow us to speak with my client. The second call will be to Mel Stiller. I'm sure you know Mel, the State Attorney of Monroe County? The purpose for that one will be to arrange a meeting for this afternoon where I will be asking him to conduct an immediate and thorough, independent investigation into this whole matter. Mel owes me one, so I have no doubt that will occur. Now, if I have to go to all of that trouble just to get to see my own client, and to obtain information on this incident here at the jail, I'm not going to be a very nice guy to deal with thereafter. Now how do you want to play it? Want to make a phone call yourself to see if these things can't happen internally, without resort to the courts?"

Deputy Superintendent Sullivan was not used to such a confrontation from a defense attorney in the confines of his own institution. He said quietly, "Wait two minutes. Let me see what I can do," and walked out the door.

In almost exactly one hundred and twenty seconds a guard came to the room and asked them to follow him. He led them to an upstairs area where Mark had never been before. At the end of a long hallway, the guard opened a large wooden door with no signs around it. That led into an anteroom where a secretary sat at a utilitarian, olive green metal desk. She stood and asked them to follow her to another door on the opposite side of the room.

She knocked once lightly, and a booming voice called from the other side: "Come in." As they entered, Mark and Jayne saw for the first time where they were. A bronze plaque was set into a stand on the desk in the center of the room, announcing the fact that they had entered into the inner sanctum of the Superintendent himself.

Superintendent Stuart Harriman came around his desk and shook hands vigorously with each of them. Jayne gave it her best effort, but her hand was crushed in Harriman's huge paw. And he was huge. At least 6'5", about 280 pounds. Looked like he had once stayed in shape.

Suicide

"So glad to meet you!" The same booming voice. A politician through and through. "I understand we have a little problem."

Seemed that everything at the institution that smacked of their ineptitude was "little," Mark thought.

"I want to clear this up as quickly as possible," Harriman continued. " I understand you need to see your client, and I'm sure you can understand we need sufficient security at the hospital to allow you to see him. This is for your protection. Also, I've already asked that written reports, from anyone who has any information about the fight, be on my desk by five o'clock today. As soon as I get them, I'll turn them over to you, so long as they don't contain any sensitive information."

Mark decided to cut in. "Superintendent, we really appreciate you seeing us so quickly, and moving on this. But we don't need protection from our own client, and we're not about to lead him in an escape attempt. So there's no reason we can't go over there right now and talk to Mr. Hunter. I also look forward to receiving the reports sometime tomorrow, but I don't know what you mean by 'sensitive' information. I don't want to see a bunch of sheets of paper where three-quarters of the text is blacked out. That won't do me any good."

"Well I'll tell you what I'm going do. I'm going to assign Officer Dooley here," and he pointed to the guard who had led them upstairs, "to accompany you to the hospital and help with security. By sensitive I meant anything that might be of a personal nature to any staff here, the other inmate involved, and the good Mr. Hunter himself. That's all. We're required by law to keep confidential certain types of information. You know that."

"Yes, I do," Mark responded. "But I don't want any games played here. We need to get to the truth."

"We will do that, I can assure you, Attorney Fitzsimmons. You can count on it."

The Superintendent called for his secretary, who led Mark and Jayne back to the attorney's room. Officer Dooley stayed behind after telling them he would meet them downstairs in a minute.

When the door closed, Harriman turned to Dooley and said in a low whisper, "I'm going to call Reilly as soon as you leave. Try to catch as much of the conversation between the three of them at the hospital as you can. We need to stonewall them as long as possible."

Dooley was out the door as the Superintendent was dialing the phone.

THIRTY-THREE

The drive to the hospital took about ten minutes. Mark knew they were being shadowed by Dooley's gray Ford with a "GOV" license plate. They had to park a distance from the main entrance, only to find Dooley standing by his car, which was parked in a handicap zone directly in front of the entrance. He led the way into the hospital and to the reception desk. Mark and Jayne were issued guest pass lapel pins and Dooley led them up the elevator to Dana's room. Another prison guard was sitting directly outside the room on a folding chair. He grunted an acknowledgement in Dooley's direction. It appeared clear he had been up all night.

Jayne was apprehensive, not knowing what she would find when they entered the room. It wasn't that bad. Dana was propped up against several pillows, watching the small TV hung in the upper corner of the room. He had gauze bandages encircling the top of his head, an IV, and slight, dark circles under his eyes, but that was it. He was overjoyed to see them.

"Hey, you guys are a sight for sore eyes! How are you?"

"Better than you, it looks like," Mark shot back with a grin.

Jayne went immediately to the side of the bed, sat on the edge, and took Dana's hand in hers. "Hi Dana," she said gently. "Are you really hurting? Tell us what happened."

"It's not too bad. The docs say I got a slight concussion. Contusions to the face. That's all. I was lucky I guess."

"Who was it?" Mark asked.

"I only know they call him Smitty," Dana replied. "One of the Irish gang that's in there. They band together against the blacks and the Cubans. It was totally unprovoked. I turned a corner in the hallway and he was there swinging at me. Got me a couple of good ones, but frankly I think he was surprised at how I fought back. I surprised myself, for God's sake. He was tough, and I had at least twenty years on him. There was some power behind me—call it what you will—anger, frustration over this whole mess. I was able to beat him back until the guards appeared—a little late, if you ask me. I got in some good licks, though."

"Had you had any prior arguments, problems with him," Jayne wanted to know.

"Nothing. Only seen him once or twice before this. May have said hello. No, I think someone put him up to it."

"I think you're right," Mark added. "But I'm going to take care of this. First, and for the immediate future, we're going to keep you here as long as possible. Then, assuming you have to go back, I'm going to make sure you're placed in protective

Suicide

custody."

"What do you mean 'assuming?' You couldn't arrange to have me stay here until the trial, could you?" Dana looked hopeful.

"Not until the trial, Dana. But we've got a couple of aces up our sleeve now. That's why we originally came to see you, thinking you were still in the jail." He then related in summary form what had happened in the police evidence room.

"The bottom line is, Dana, you weren't wearing the shirt on which they found the gunpowder. And our expert is certain that shirt couldn't have gotten the residue on it by simple contact with other clothing. That means someone fired a gun near that shirt. And it wasn't you, I'm sure."

Dana's face showed a mixture of delight and confusion. "So what does this mean, Mark? Are you saying the residue was planted on my T-shirt? Who would have done that?"

"Taking your last question first, I don't know who would have done it, but I certainly have my suspicions. Yes, I firmly believe the shirt was intentionally exposed to gunpowder. Exactly how, I can't say right now. There is one other question that I hope you can answer. The sleeveless shirt you wore that day wasn't in any of the bags, and I know they took all of your clothing. Do you have any idea where it is?"

Dana paused, deep in thought. "I came home. I remember

I was very sweaty. Drenched, in fact. I took off my clothes. I usually would hang them on the edge of the laundry basket or hamper so they would dry before they sat in a heap somewhere. I know I took a shower—"

"What else, Dana?" Jayne inquired. She was encouraging him to prompt his memory. "Think hard."

"I now remember I noticed how bad I smelled. That hasn't happened to me in a long time. I remember thinking it was because of the stress of the incident, the questioning by the police . . . all of that." Then Dana added rhetorically: "What in the heck did I do with that shirt?"

Jayne, in jest, gave her own answer. "If I had been there you would have thrown it in the trash, or I would have beaten you alongside your head."

It was as if a light went on inside Dana's head. "Wait! I know. What you just said Jayne. I did throw the damn thing away. In one of the large trash barrels by the side of the apartment building. They collect and cart it away twice a week. It's long gone in the garbage dump."

"Well, that's the answer then," Mark interjected. "I guess it would be better to have it to show conclusively that it had no gunpowder on it, but at least it's beyond the reach of anyone else who might want to plant residue on it."

"That's good," Jayne and Dana said simultaneously, giving

each other sheepish grins.

    Just then Mark noticed out of the corner of his eye that the door to the room was slightly ajar, and Officer Dooley was standing right next to it. He walked over and closed it sharply with a bang.

    "We don't need anybody else in on our conversation." Mark moved over closer to the bed and began speaking in a whisper.

    "OK, here's the plan. I'm going to file an emergency motion with the court to do two things: one, place all of the evidence in the hands of a neutral commissioner. Not a typical motion, but one which I think, under the circumstances, has a good chance of success. Second, to review all of the videotape and logs of the evidence room since the date of the search of your place. Lastly, I'm also going to ask the court to review the issue of your bail because of this new evidence. With any luck, we might be able to get the bail reduced to a point where you can make it."

    "Mark, I can't thank you enough," Dana said with tears in his eyes. "I've been wracking my brain ever since this whole thing started as to how the gunpowder got on my shirt. I never suspected it wasn't the shirt I was wearing that day. Frankly, I couldn't remember which shirt it was. That's the only one that is cut off. I did it because the sleeves were getting so frayed. Lucky thing I had it on that day."

"I appreciate the thanks, but it's my job. Let's keep our fingers crossed on the motions."

The three of them spoke for a few more minutes. Jayne finally told Dana about her excitement the prior night. Dana was flabbergasted: both out of concern for her safety, and that she would come to see him the morning after being attacked and killing a man. Jayne was one tough cookie, Dana thought. But she also had a marvelous feminine, sensitive side. What a great combo.

Mark took his leave, wanting to get back to work on the motions. Jayne and Dana remained alone in the room.

"Jayne, are you sure you're all right? That must have been a terrible experience."

"I'm OK. It all happened so fast I'm not sure it even happened at all. But I know it did. I think it will hit me in a few days. I haven't had to go back to my place yet, and maybe that's a good thing. I'm just more concerned about you now. That you're going to be OK."

"I'll be fine. I feel that I'm in good hands with you and Mark. You're really fighting for me."

"That's because we feel a terrible injustice is being done here. And the fact that there might be police complicity, or at least a cover-up, makes it all the worse."

"That's what scares the crap out of me as well. I had a bad feeling from my first exchange with Reilly and Santos, assuming they're the ones who are involved in this. I didn't exactly get off on my best foot with them either. I have to tell you Jayne, this whole experience has already caused some major changes in me. I can feel it." Dana put his hand on Jayne's and looked her directly in the eye.

"For one, and I hate to admit this to you, but I've been pretty much a homophobe all my life. My dad was pretty bad. You know, fag this, queer that. That's what I was exposed to. A real false sense of machismo. False, because you had to act more macho than you really were. My contact with Mark has caused me to examine that side of myself very carefully. And I can honestly say I've done a one-eighty on it. He's a man I can rely upon, put all my trust and faith in. In fact, he's twice the man I'll ever be."

"Mark is a great man," Jayne said as she gave Dana's hand a squeeze. I've worked for him long enough to know that. His sexuality has nothing to do with his character. As a woman, I'm especially sensitive to that. Too many times I've seen people pre-judge me because I'm a woman. When I was a teenager, guys were actually shocked to find I could out-argue them, fix a car, and shoot better than they could. Didn't have many dates in those years. Now I tend to like older men," and here Jayne gave Dana a flutter of a wink, "because I find them more accepting of my being a strong person. Note I didn't say strong 'woman'.

Older guys have seen enough to know women are their equals while still celebrating 'la difference.'"

"Well, with you, Jayne, I certainly celebrate that difference," Dana said, giving back a clearer wink. "The fact is, I like strong women . . . ah, people," Dana added with a smile. "But I think now we have to focus on staying safe, and resolving this case. For all of us. It would kill me if you, or Mark, or anyone associated with you was harmed as a result of me. Let's not let that happen."

"We won't, Dana, we won't. We're now on guard, Let 'em come at us. We can give as well as we can get."

"That a girl, Jayne," Dana said with mock bravado. "But on a more serious note, let's be careful out there, as they used to say on that cop show."
"Hill Street Blues. I still catch those re-runs every so often. Greatest cop show in history, if you ask me," Jayne said.

"Yeah, let's be careful out there. Funny that we're the civilians, and we have to say that."

"Yeah, funny," Dana said.

THIRTY-FOUR

When Mark got back to the office, he immediately put in a call to Tommy, who answered on the second ring.

"Hey my man, how's it goin'?" Tommy said.

"Not bad. 'Bout you?"

"Hangin' in there. Trying to stay outta' trouble."

"Yeah, I know that one. Any success?"

"Nope. Met a nice girl last night, though."

Tommy's womanizing was well-known.

"So how long will she last? Last night?"

"Very funny bro. I'm gonna' surprise you and get married one of these days," Tommy said with a chuckle.

"OK if I don't hold my breath, man?"

"Now, now, we can all change. But you're right. Doesn't seem too likely now. So what's up?"

"I'm a little worried about our boy. He got assaulted yesterday at the jail and is in the hospital. It could have been just a random attack, but I don't think so. I also didn't like the tone of the Superintendent's voice when I met with him about it. Just a trace of sarcasm there."

"Was he hurt badly?"

"Not too bad. Slight concussion, some scrapes and bruises. I think our guy's tougher than we think. But I don't want it to happen again. Next time could be a lot worse."

"Is he being guarded at the hospital?"

"He is, by a prison guard. I just don't trust the whole situation. Think you could arrange to stop by every so often? Let your presence be known. At different times so they won't know when to expect you."

"Easy. I'll run over there this afternoon and evening. And then late at night. Will that do it?"

"For now. Then we'll reassess the situation. Thanks Tommy. I really appreciate it. Just add it to the tab."

"No problemo, bro. It's as good as done."

Tommy did as he said. He made a big production of seeing Dana, showing his investigator's license to everyone who would look, including the guard. Mark had already emailed a letter to the prison and the hospital announcing that Tommy worked for him. It was also fortuitous that Tommy had dated one of the head nurses on the floor, who still held a flame for him.

The guard was a little tense when he saw Tommy was packing a .38, which he carried with him everywhere. Right out in the open where everyone could see it, especially the guard. He visited twice, at 1:00 and 6:00 PM. Went into the room, shot the shit with Dana for a bit each time, and then told everyone

Suicide

in a loud voice that he wouldn't be back until the next morning. Little did they know he meant 3:00 AM in the morning.

Tommy knew a back way in where he could avoid the check-in procedure at the main desk. He had discovered it when he and the nurse had satisfied their desires in a janitor's closet in a remote area in the basement of the hospital. At around 2:50 A.M., he found a poorly latched window that afforded him ingress to the area. It still required him to slither on his stomach through a small opening. From there he could drop a few feet into a storage room and make his way up the back stairs to Dana's floor.

When he quietly opened the door onto the area, he took a quick right and then a left, which he knew would put him right within thirty feet of Dana's room. As he rounded the second corner, he was shocked to see no one in the chair outside the room. Probably just a bathroom break, he thought. But still, they should have called up someone from security men to take over for those few minutes.

Tommy quietly approached the room, and suddenly saw some movement on the other side of the curtained window that was just to the side of the door. The door was shut. He softly pushed the handle down and the door opened with a click. The startled guard was standing over Dana with a small hypodermic needle in his right hand. Dana was sound asleep.

"Drop that fuckin' thing right now, asshole," Tommy shouted as he pulled out his gun with one smooth motion. The guard hesitated momentarily, and then dropped the syringe to the floor, where it shattered into small fragments.

"I was just giving him his sedative," the man said with a slight stutter.

"Yeah right! Now move away from him. Slowly. If I see your hands go anywhere but up in the air, you're gonna' have six holes in you in one second flat."

The guard moved away, his hands out away from his body. Then he began to protest in earnest. "Put that goddamn gun away. Do you realize who you're talking to? I'm on the prison staff as an authorized law enforcement official. You're pulling a gun on a cop, asshole. I'd suggest you put that thing away before you get yourself into deeper shit."

Tommy kept the weapon trained directly on the man's heart, and pulled back the hammer with a loud click when the guard started to let his hands drop.

"I think you were just about to commit a murder, Mr. law enforcement officer. But we'll let the real police resolve that one." Tommy slid his cell phone out of his pocket with his other hand and dialed 911. He calmly reported a possible homicide attempt at the hospital, and gave the room number.

He stayed on the phone until the police arrived just two

minutes later. Luckily, they had been behind an ambulance which had been pulling into the emergency area just as Tommy had surprised the guard. The man didn't try anything except to attempt to talk his way out of the situation again. Tommy wasn't buying it for a second. The cops came in the door, guns drawn. Tommy lowered his .38 to the floor at their command. There were two of them, and they now had their weapons pointed at both Tommy and the guard.

The commotion finally awakened Dana, who lifted his body with a start when he groggily perceived what was going on. The man was yelling loudly now that he had to get back to the jail pronto—they were short-staffed—his supervisor would be pissed. But when he couldn't produce any evidence he was in fact a guard at the jail—and when the nurses and doctors who entered the room after they heard all the noise and saw the cops arrive affirmed that this guy had no authority to administer anything, much less with a needle—the police placed him under arrest. One of the doctors picked up the glass pieces, and informed the police that since there was no medication on the floor, the most the man could have pumped into Dana's body was a string of air bubbles, which would most assuredly have stopped his heart.

Tommy placed a call to Mark, who arrived in an astonishing fifteen minutes considering the time of night. It didn't take much to get the shift supervisor at the station to authorize a police detail to guard Dana for the foreseeable future. Things calmed down a bit, and Mark and the police got the full story from Tommy. Dana thanked them profusely for saving his life.

When it was just Mark, Tommy and Dana left, they began to talk quietly between them. Dana spoke first. "Mark, what do you think is going on here? Why does someone want to kill me? Is Holmes' family behind this? Is it revenge? I just can't figure this out."

"I don't think it's the family," Mark replied. "The widow just doesn't seem like the kind who would pursue this. Their children are out of state and hardly equipped to orchestrate everything that's happened. I mean, here's what we've got. Our first good witness, Michael, is suddenly visited by the police, who suggest in no uncertain terms that he should leave the state. Benzedrine swears that Reilly and Santos put him up to concocting a story. Then Jayne is attacked by an ex-cop who was run off the force. There's powder stains on a shirt you weren't even wearing that day. And now these attacks on you when you're supposed to be under guard. No, I think all the evidence points to Reilly and Santos, or other police officers.

"In about five hours I'm going to be laying all this out to the judge on those emergency motions I was telling you about. I just hope this latest attempt on you was not precipitated by my motions. I had to drop off copies to the prosecutor's office late

Suicide

in the day, and given the explosive allegations contained in the papers, I'm sure his first phone call was to the chief. No question the Detectives knew what was coming down. As to why they're doing it, I just can't say. It's my job right now to make sure you're protected."

"Protect me from the police, Mark. How are you going to do that? I've got to tell you I'm pretty scared right now."

"I'd be less than honest if I didn't tell you I wasn't scared either. But we've got the resources, and the law, to fight them with, and fight them we will. Stay strong Dana. We'll get to the bottom of this."

"I have no doubt you will," Dana replied. "Just so long as I'm not at the bottom of the ocean when that happens."

THIRTY-FIVE

Mark appeared in court at exactly nine that morning, feeling no ill effects from the early hour awakening that had forced him to the hospital. He was simply too wired to feel anything. Jayne was with him to take over the second chair.

They were both a little surprised to see not only Bob Delaney, the assistant prosecutor who had been assigned the case, but Mel Stiller, the State Attorney of the Keys, and two other underlings. *I guess they're taking this pretty seriously,* Mark thought. But no Reilly or Santos. He gave them but a peremptory wave of the hand. This was war.

He had been told by the judge's session clerk that he would be heard on his motions after two other brief matters were addressed. In addition to the larger than usual prosecution team, the gallery was packed with lawyers and members of the public at large. Apparently, word had gotten out that something big was going to happen in the Hunter murder case. Courtrooms are often like accident scenes—rubber neckers are always going to be available to catch some gore. The tension in the courtroom was palpable.

Dana was brought in by two court officers. By

Suicide

prearrangement, they removed the shackles and allowed him to sit at the defense table in between Mark and Jayne.

Judge Harvey came out and took his seat at the dais. Mark knew when he was settled he always gave a hearty good morning to everyone in his courtroom. The good cheer was short lived, however—although scrupulously fair, the Judge was a hard man who did not suffer fools gladly. As an attorney, Mark knew he had to get to the point swiftly and stay there. Harvey's reputation for berating loquacious attorneys was well-known.

As predicted, two brief motions were heard first, but still an hour had passed, so the Judge took a short morning recess. To Mark's surprise, it turned into a half-hour break, unusual for Harvey's tightly-run ship. Mark hoped he was reviewing the pleadings before coming out.

He had given him a lot to digest—affidavits from Michael containing a brief synopsis of his expected testimony on Holmes; from Tommy on Benny's recantation and allegations of police abuse; another from Stephen Weeks, verifying that the two eight by ten glossy photographs of Dana were true and accurate depictions of him and the crime scene; and of course, last but hardly least, a sworn statement from Walter outlining his findings relative to the T-shirt. Also included was a memorandum of law tying in specific appellate decisions supporting Mark's request for the appointment of a commissioner to hold and protect the evidence, and to lower Dana's bail.

But Mark knew it was naive to believe a trial court judge like Harvey, with his incredibly busy schedule, would have fully digested the information presented to him before actually hearing from the attorneys. Usually he would allow the advocates to explain the facts and the issues to him before retiring to do a personal review of the documentation.

So he was surprised when Harvey, visibly agitated, bellowed at the prosecutorial side of the room. Addressing specifically the assistant prosecutor, he said, "Mr. Delaney, have you had an opportunity to review all of Mr. Fitzsimmons' paperwork?"

"Your Honor," Delaney spoke querulously. "I've only had last night. All of this was delivered to our office at five PM yesterday. My first request is for a brief continuance of this hearing, say two to three days, so we can fully review these allegations and properly answer them."

"There will be no continuance, Mr. Delaney." The judge said his name slowly, in three distinct syllables: Dee ... lane ... ey."

Mark had never seen him so sarcastic and demeaning. He didn't have long to wait to see worse.

"We're going to get to the bottom of this today, here in my courtroom. Is that understood, Mr. Dee ... lane ... ey?"

Suicide

The prosecutor was holding onto the table in front of him for support. His previously whining tone was supplanted by a tremulous, high-pitched screech. "Yes, I understand Your Honor."

"Now, where are Detectives Reilly and Santos?" the Judge demanded.

"They're in Miami. Actually looking for Mr. Benny Hopkins, a key witness in this case, who mysteriously disappeared about a month ago. They've been there for two days, and haven't had time to come back."

"Well, that's convenient, Mr. Delaney. You mean the same Mr. Hopkins, about whom I have an affidavit? The one who purportedly was beaten into giving false testimony by those two detectives? Are we talking about the same person, Mr. Dee ... lane ... ey?"

"Well, Your Honor. Those are just allegations. I'm sure the Detectives will be happy to clarify the matter."

"Well, they're not here now, are they Mr. Delaney? It's a three-hour drive from Miami to Key West. Maybe four with bad traffic. If it were me, and allegations such as these were made against me, I sure as hell would have my ass sittin' right here in this courtroom, and I'd be explaining myself."

Mark had never heard Judge Harvey swear in his court. This was fun to watch—so long as things didn't turn and he became the object of the court's wrath. He didn't.

Harvey was just getting started. He went through the evidence laid out in the papers piece by piece and asked the prosecutor to refute each element of them. When he couldn't, at one point stating he thought the photographs were doctored, the Judge

blew up. "Mr. Dee ... lane ... ey. As an officer of this court, are you telling me you have any proof—any whatsoever—that these photos have been altered or tampered with?"

"Well . . . ah . . . no proof. But we haven't had enough time to test them," the prosecutor said meekly.

"Well, I'll tell you this Mr. Delaney," the Judge roared. "Mr. Weeks has been in my court for many years reporting on our judicial proceedings. He has been an objective, well-respected journalist in these parts for the same amount of time. Not only that, Mr. Dee ... lane ... ey. He's my wife's first cousin. He's attended many of our family functions. Are you telling me today that my wife's cousin is a liar, and perjurer, who would make false sworn statements to this court? Is that what you're saying?"

This couldn't get any better, Mark thought. He had no idea Steven Weeks was related to the Judge.

When Mr. Delaney assured the court that he was certain the cousin was not as described, Judge Harvey completed his questioning, and turned calmly toward Mark. The transformation

<u>Suicide</u>

was astonishingly quick.

"Is there anything you would like to add to these proceedings, Mr. Fitzsimmons?"

Mark addressed the final issue, which had not been taken up at this point—the attacks on the legal team and Dana. He outlined in detail what they knew so far. The outrage perpetrated upon Jayne, by an ex-cop of all people. The two assaults on Dana, both at times when he was supposed to be protected by the state. He related that the ersatz guard had refused to say a word and had immediately demanded an attorney. One was on his way from Fort Lauderdale. Nobody could figure why he had to reach that far away.

Harvey listened with serious attention. Finally, he called another recess, telling the litigants that they should hang tight. He was going to make a decision on at least some of the motions that morning before the lunch break.

THIRTY-SIX

They had finally found him. Reilly had pulled out all the stops on this one. He was in the North Beach area of Miami Beach. Had been hanging around the North Shore Park. Benny was immediately taken into custody on trumped up charges until the Detective could get up there.

Once he did, it didn't take long before Benny spilled his guts about how he had ended up there. Reilly now sensed what he was fully up against. That sense became a firm conviction when he got a call from Delaney that next evening describing the allegations in Mark's pleadings.

His first call was to Charlie, the desk Sergeant on duty that night.

"Charlie, this is Reilly. Who else is there?"

"It's me and Hoffman. Then the guys on the street."

"OK. Let me speak to Hoffman."

Glenn Hoffman, a twenty-year fixture on the force, picked up immediately.

"Hey Reill's. Whasss up?"

"Finally located Benzedrine. He's secure. Hey. I need a small favor. Can you go into the evidence room? There's one bag

Suicide

marked with yellow tape—It's the only one—amongst the Hunter evidence. Grab it and put it in my office. Lock my door behind you too."

"Reill's, you know I'd do anything for ya. But my hands are tied. Along with everyone else's. The room is buttoned up as tight as an old maid's pussy. Just this evening the chief got some local security guys to come in, change and add locks to the room, and alarm it. Don't know why. It's the craziest thing I've seen here. Ever."

Reilly could barely control his outrage—and his fear. He had rarely been afraid in his life. Confronting a perp with a handgun, or a barroom brawl, just got his juices flowing. Too fast to feel any emotion. Now he was overwhelmed with a foreboding that events were accelerating beyond his control.

He had to take control again. Fast.

THIRTY-SEVEN

Justice Robert Harvey came out and took the bench at precisely 12:45, fifteen minutes before the usual time for the lunch break. He looked especially severe. And that was saying something. There was no friendly greeting this time. He addressed the parties, but his voice could be heard even in the far recesses of the court room.

"For the record, it's Friday, November 16, 2007. Before me is the matter of the State versus Dana Hunter, Docket No. 07-8492. The defendant filed certain motions with the court yesterday afternoon, and because of the emergency nature of those motions, as supported by numerous affidavits and exhibits, I agreed to hear them this morning with short notice to the State. I denied the State's verbal motion to continue this hearing on the same basis, that is, I believed the motions to be of sufficient urgency to warrant an expedited hearing."

The judge paused momentarily, as if to further gather his thoughts. Dana fidgeted in his seat until Mark put his hand calmly on his shoulder.

"Before me is a motion to appoint a special commissioner

Suicide

to take custody, possession and control of all evidence held by the State in this matter. The second is a motion to reduce, or eliminate bail. Do both parties agree that those are the motions before me?"

Mark and the prosecutor stood and said, almost in unison, "Yes, Your Honor."

"All right. The motion to appoint a commissioner is granted. I believe there is sufficient evidence of the possibility that the State has engaged in improper conduct to warrant the safeguarding of that evidence. I have already spoken personally with the Chief of Police and he has assured me the evidence is secure and will remain that way until the commissioner can take possession of it. So, I hereby appoint Attorney Roger Bellow as special commissioner in this matter, with full power and authority to safeguard all evidence in this case in whatever way necessary, until further order of this court. Does either party have a specific objection to Attorney Bellow serving in this capacity?"

Mark knew Roger Bellow very well. He had been a lawyer in the Keys for as long as Mark could remember, and had an excellent reputation. He was also known as a good golfing and drinking buddy of the Judge's. Mark signified his lack of any objection with a quick "No, Your Honor." The prosecutor, wisely as Mark thought, did the same.

"Fine," Judge Harvey continued. "Let us move onto the

next motion, the motion regarding bail. The reason for the recess was that I wanted to check on a couple of statutes and cases."

Gesturing toward an attractive young lady sitting next to the clerk just below the dais, he said, "I also want to thank my law clerk, Emily, for her great assistance in that endeavor."

Mark was aware there had been a few rumors floating around the court house about the exact nature of Judge Harvey's relationship with this particular law clerk, and several in the past as well. It was well known that Judge Harvey somehow ended up with female clerks, all young and voluptuous, although the appointments were supposed to be random.

"I am confident the law does not permit me, as much as I may want to, to vacate all bail in a first-degree murder case, or to release a defendant so charged on his personal recognizance."

Dana took a deep breath as he heard this, expecting the worst. It looked like he was going to be a denizen of the prison system for the time being.

"But that does not end the matter," Harvey went on. "The case law also gives me the power, *sua sponte*, that is, entirely on my own, without any motion before me, to dismiss a criminal charge where, based on the evidence presented, there is a substantial likelihood that a miscarriage of justice is being perpetrated, and no other remedy will resolve that injustice. I find that to be the case here."

A wide smile spread across Mark's face. Dana did not understand quite what the judge was saying, but he sensed it was good for him, given the State Attorney's look of total dejection, and Mark's ebullience.

"Therefore, I am hereby dismissing the charge of murder against Mr. Hunter here, without prejudice to the State, which may bring the charges again, but only if they demonstrate by a preponderance of the evidence that they have additional, untainted facts sufficient to convince me the charges may be reinstated. Mr. Hunter, you are hereby released from custody."

A cry of joy erupted from Jayne's throat before she could suppress it. They all stood and did a group hug. Everyone was sobbing. Some in the gallery broke out in spontaneous clapping. It was the happiest moment in Dana's life.

When things had quieted a bit, and Mark had packed his briefcase and they were ready to leave, Tommy came up to Mark, pulled him slightly aside, and whispered in his ear. The smile disappeared from Mark's countenance. Dana looked questioningly at Mark. He asked him what was the matter?

Mark said in a low whisper, "When we leave here, we're all getting separate rooms at the Crowne Plaza for a couple of nights—under Tommy's name. He's already made the arrangements."

"C'mon Mark," Dana said. "I haven't been home in three months. What's this all about?"

"Dana, you're going to have to trust me this one more time. We need to stay out of sight for a while. This isn't over."

With that Tommy and Mark grabbed Dana's and Jayne's arms respectively and hurried them out of the court room.

THIRTY-EIGHT

They all took up residence at the Crowne on Duval under Tommy's name. Mark explained to Dana and Jayne that Tommy's "associates" had found out that the police had located Benny. The word was also out on the street that Reilly was out for revenge. It was better to lay low right now until Mark could look into the matter and possibly get protection for them. He did have some contacts within the FBI.

After three days, they were going stir crazy. It was a Friday, and late that afternoon Mark had arranged a secret meeting with his Fed contact at his office. He wouldn't let Jayne or Dana come with him.

There was a bar at the top of the hotel with a patio that afforded the best aerial views in the City. Sunset came at 6:37 that evening, and Dana and Jayne decided to watch it from the roof deck. Mark thought it would be fine so long as they remained in a very public spot. There was a folk/rock trio playing music. Generally light stuff, like James Taylor, C, S N & Y. It was a beautiful night. They were two glasses of Chardonnay into it when the top tip of the flaming orange globe slid into the sea.

"What an awesome sight," Jayne sighed. "I wish this

moment could last forever."

"I do too," Dana replied as he admired the way the pinkish hues softened Jayne's features and danced in her hair. "These last three days have only been bearable because I've been able to spend so much time with you."

"I feel the same way Dana. It's allowed me to get to know you even better. And what I see, I like. A lot."

Dana instinctively leaned down and gently kissed Jayne on the lips. He only intended it to be a soft peck, the embarrassment of the first kiss preventing him from seeking to extend it. But Jayne did. She opened her mouth wider, pressing slightly back at him, until the kiss evolved into a deep, hungry searching of each other's souls. They parted, realizing that this was not the time or place for more, but each knowing there would be. Later.

THIRTY-NINE

Mark left the meeting much more optimistic about the near future. Len, a fifteen-year veteran of the FBI, had prior to arriving at Mark's office thoroughly reviewed the evidence pointing to police misconduct. He told Mark that he had authority from the Regional Director to assemble a team to investigate the matter fully—even to offer protection to those who needed it. Because that would entail safe houses, and constant moving about, Mark declined for the time being. He would discuss the option with Jayne and Dana.

Len showed Mark a draft of a subpoena which the United States Attorney intended to serve upon the Key West Police Department by the end of the week. It sought, among other items, copies of all videotapes and logs relating to the evidence room during the salient period of time.

So Mark was euphoric, believing now that the pressure put to bear on the cops by the Feds would chill any attempts at retribution, or re-opening the case against Dana. He decided to walk home to get some exercise and fresh air after the last few days in the increasingly cramped hotel room. It was just getting dark.

FORTY

Jayne and Dana were sitting side by side now at the upstairs bar, their hands intertwined. They had spoken more easily now of the events of the past months, as if a single kiss had opened the floodgates of emotions that had been contained for so long. They cuddled and laughed, oblivious to the few patrons around them who occasionally stole a glance at their happiness. Finally, they decided to call it a night, probably one or two glasses of wine too late. Both were a bit unsteady as they made their way into the elevator and descended to their rooms.

The evening was as gentle as a Key West evening could be. A soft, warm breeze ruffled his hair and kissed his bare arms. He couldn't wait to get home and see Brad, who had only been able to visit once at the hotel because of work demands. Mark did, out of a seeming excess of caution, occasionally check behind him to make sure no one was following.

As he turned the corner onto Leon Street, just a block from home, a hooded figure calmly stepped out from behind a bush and pointed his finger at him. It wasn't until the barbed hook struck his chest, and the thirty thousand volts of electricity coursed through his body, that Mark realized it wasn't a finger,

Suicide

but a taser, the man held. Mark had never felt such debilitating pain. His whole body, flesh, organs, every inch, caught on fire. He fell, writhing, unable to utter a word.

Even when the charge abated, Mark lay motionless, although now fully conscious, the electric jolt having temporarily rendered his muscles useless. The figure approached him with a hypodermic needle held between his fingers. Flashes of the attempt on Dana's life crowded his mind.

"This won't hurt a bit, fag-boy," the man whispered, a touch of glee in his voice. He lowered the needle to inject Mark in the arm. Mark was helpless to even cry out, much less avoid the impending syringe. As the sharp point was just pushing into Mark's arm, but not yet puncturing the skin, a series of sharp cracks came from behind him, and the figure blew backward as if magically carried by some unknown force. Mark watched, as a spectator in a dream, as Tommy approached the figure, his still hot gun held firmly in his hand and pointed at the now prostrate body on the sidewalk. The hood had fallen back behind the man's head. Detective Reilly's face was contorted into a death mask.

FORTY-ONE

Tommy didn't bill Mark for the extra time he had spent tailing him that night. That was a labor of love. But he did get a very nice Christmas bonus.

It didn't take long for the Special Task Force of the Federal Bureau of Investigation to uncover the misconduct. Despite his best efforts to conceal the shirt, a high definition re-work of the evidence room videotape clearly revealed Reilly furtively tucking it inside his jacket. His presence in the room, and return after visiting the firing range, was supported by the written log book.

Dana's attacker at the hospital, when he finally no longer had to fear Reilly's wrath, spilled his guts about Reilly's promise of twenty-five thousand dollars for the deed when certain life insurance monies came in. Of course, they never did. The insurance company got the complete federal investigative report, and denied coverage based on the clear and convincing evidence of the suicide, and the desperate attempts to turn it into a murder.

Dana and Jayne moved together up further in the Keys to Islamorada. Mark, Brad and Tommy attended their wedding there. Dana became a successful author, while Jayne spent her time trying her hand at painting and sculpture, from which she made a modest income.

Rusty Hodgdon

Mark had no permanent ill effects from the taser. His business boomed as a result of the publicity over the Hunter case. At least once a month the two couples would take turns visiting each other. No mention of the case was ever made during those visits.

About the Author

Rusty Hodgdon is a graduate of Yale University where he majored in English Literature and Creative Writing. After graduating with a Juris Doctor degree from the Boston University School of Law, he practiced law for over twenty years in the Boston area, first as a Public Defender, then with his own firm. He left the practice of law and moved to Key West Florida to pursue his passion to write creative fiction. Rusty is also the winner of the 2012 Key West Mystery Fest Short Story contest. All comments are welcome. Write to him at RUSTY.THE.WRITER@GMAIL.COM

Made in the USA
Columbia, SC
16 November 2018